I0661589

Alfred Austin

Narrative poems

Alfred Austin

Narrative poems

ISBN/EAN: 9783744708326

Printed in Europe, USA, Canada, Australia, Japan

Cover: Foto ©Andreas Hilbeck / pixelio.de

More available books at **www.hansebooks.com**

NARRATIVE POEMS

BY

ALFRED AUSTIN

London

MACMILLAN AND CO.

AND NEW YORK

1891

All rights reserved

DEDICATION

TO

SIR JOHN EVERETT MILLAIS, R.A., BART.

My dear Millais,

In tendering you the dedication of this little volume, with Florence basking below me in the sunshine, and within an arrowshot of the villa where Lorenzo died, this very day, close on four hundred years ago, I am vividly reminded of that Renaissance of Art with which their names are for ever associated, and which, after a ·brief span of dignity and splendour, lapsed into florid effeminacy and social degradation.

In your brilliant boyhood there occurred in our own land an Æsthetic Revival, and with the sensitiveness of genius you experienced its attractive and, within proper limits, its salutary influence. There are those, I am told, who reproach you, because, in the gradual development of your powers, you liberated yourself from its sway. To me, it seems, it is your distinctive and abiding glory.

In Art, as in life, and whether the art be painting, poetry, or music, there is the masculine element, and there is the feminine element. Both are good, but surely only on condition that the masculine element predominates. The feminine note is a lovely note, an indispensable note; but it should be the pathetic minor, not the dominant key.

Something of the masculinity of your work must be attributed to your own robust nature. But, in common with more than one of your contemporaries whose productions have added grace and lustre to the Victorian Era, you doubtless owe it, in the main, to the indestructible manliness of our race. There is no fear lest English painting, or English literature, should decline into a languid æstheticism; or that, subjugated by a feminine fondness for detail and lack of breadth, we should forget to allot to the various influences that underlie life, and that minister to art, their due place and proportion.

It is interesting to note that, thoroughly English painter as you are, you have been instinctively drawn

to the instructive companionship and loving delineation
of external nature, so that your loveliest canvases seem
to savour of the heather and to resound with the
brawl of mountain torrents. There lies the cure and
corrective of that paralysing despondency which is en-
gendered by the incessant nervous activity of urban
existence. There lurks the source and sustenance of
that cheerful gravity which extracts from life its soundest
interpretation, and which invests painting with a nobility
of aspect that more than atones for the inevitable
absence of moral purpose.

Believe me, My dear Millais,

With cordial greeting,

Yours very sincerely,

ALFRED AUSTIN.

La Casa Nuova, Careggi,
April 7, 1891.

CONTENTS

A DIALOGUE AT FIESOLE

HE

HALT here awhile. That mossy-cushioned seat
Is for your queenliness a natural throne ;
As I am fitly couched on this low sward,
Here at your feet.

SHE

           And I, in thought, at yours ;
My adoration, deepest.

HE

           Deep, so deep,
I have no thought wherewith to fathom it ;
Or, shall I say, no flight of song so high,
To reach the Heaven whence you look down on me,
My star, my far-off star !

SHE

           If far, yet fixed :
No shifting planet leaving you to seek
Where now it shines.

B   N

HE

A little light, if near,
Glows livelier than the largest orb in Heaven.

SHE

But little lights burn quickly out, and then,
Another must be kindled.   Stars gleam on,
Unreached, but unextinguished. . . . Now, the song.

HE

Yes, yes, the song : your music to my verse.

SHE

In this sequestered dimple of the hill,
Forgotten by the furrow, none will hear :
Only the nightingales, that misconceive
The mid-day darkness of the cypresses
For curtained night.

HE

And they will hush to hear
A sudden singing sweeter than their own.
Delay not the enchantment, but begin.

SHE (*singing*)

If you were here, if you were here,
The cattle-bells would sound more clear ;

The cataracts would flash and leap
More silvery from steep to steep ;
The farewell of a rosier glow
Soften the summit of the snow ;
The valley take a tenderer green ;
In dewy gorge and dim ravine
The loving bramble-flowers embrace
The rough thorn with a gentler grace ;
The gentian open bluer eyes,
In bluer air, to bluer skies :
The frail anemone delay,
The jonquil hasten on its way,
The primrose linger past its time,
The violet prolong its prime ;
And every flower that seeks the light,
On Alpine lowland, Alpine height,
Wear April's smile without its tear,
If you were here ; if you were here !

If you were here, the Spring would wake
A fuller music in the brake.
The mottled misselthrush would pipe
A note more ringing, rich, and ripe ;
The whitethroat peer above its nest
With brighter eye and downier breast ;
The cuckoo greet the amorous year,
Chanting its joy without its jeer ;
The lark betroth the earth and sky
With peals of heavenlier minstrelsy ;
And every wildwood bird rejoice

On fleeter wing, with sweeter voice,
If you were here !

If you were here, I too should feel
The moisture of the Springtide steal
Along my veins, and rise and roll
Through every fibre of my soul.
In my live breast would melt the snow,
And all its channels flush and flow
With waves of life and streams of song,
Frozen and silent all too long.
A something in each wilding flower,
Something in every scented shower,
Something in flitting voice and wing,
Would drench my heart and bid me sing :
Not in this feeble halting note,
But, like the merle's exulting throat,
With carol full and carol clear,
If you were here, if you were here.

HE

Hark !   How the hills have caught the strain, and seem
Loth to surrender it, and now enclose
Its cadence in the silence of their folds.
Still as you sang, the verses had the wing
Of that which buoyed them, and your aery voice
Lifted my drooping music from the ground.
Now that you cease, there is an empty nest,
From which the full-fledged melody hath flown.

SHE

Dare I with you contend in metaphor,
It might not be so fanciful to show
That nest, and eggs, and music, all are yours.
But modesty in poets is too rare,
To be reproved for error.　Let me then
Be crowned full queen of song, albeit in sooth
I am but consort, owing my degree
To the real sceptred Sovereign at my side.
But now repay my music, and in kind ;
Unfolding to my ear the youngest flower
Of song that seems to blossom all the year ;
" Delay not the enchantment, but begin."

HE (*reciting*)

Yet, you are here ; yes, you are here.
There's not a voice that wakes the year,
In vale frequented, upland lone,
But steals some sweetness from your own.
When dream and darkness have withdrawn,
I feel you in the freshening dawn :
You fill the noonday's hushed repose ;
You scent the dew of daylight's close.
The twilight whispers you are nigh ;
The stars announce you in the sky.
The moon, when most alone in space,
Fills all the heavens with your face.
In darkest hour of deepest night,

A DIALOGUE AT FIESOLE

I see you with the spirit's sight ;
And slumber murmurs in my ear,
" Hush ! she is here.   Sleep ! she is here."

SHE

Hark how you bare your secret when you sing !
Imagination's universal scope
Can swift endue this gray and shapeless world
With the designs and colour of the sky.
What want you with our fixed and lumpish forms,
You, unconditioned arbiter of air ?
"Yet, you are here ; yes, you are here."   The span
Of nimble fancy leaps the interval,
And brings the distant nearer than the near.

HE

Distance is nearer than proximity,
When distance longs, proximity doth not.

SHE

The near is always distant to the mind
That craves for satisfaction of its end ;
Nor doth the distance ever feel so far
As when the end is touched.   Retard that goal,
Prolonging appetite beyond the feast
That feeds anticipation.

HE

Specious foil !
That parries every stroke before 'tis made.
Yet surfeit's self doth not more surely cloy
Than endless fasting.

SHE

Still a swifter cure
Waits on too little than attends too much.
While disappointment merely woundeth Hope,
The deadly blow by disenchantment dealt
Strikes at the heart of Faith.　O happy you,
The favourites of Fancy, who replace
Illusion with illusion, and conceive
Fresh cradles in the dark womb of the grave.
While we, prosaic victims, prove that time
Kills love while leaving loveless life alive,
You still, divinely duped, sing deathless love,
And with your wizard music, once again,
Make Winter Spring.　Yet surely you forgive
That I have too much pity for the flowers
Children and poets cull to fling away,
To be an April nosegay.

HE

How you swell
The common chorus !　Women, who are wronged
So roughly by men's undiscerning word,
As though one pattern served to show them all,

Should be more just to poets.   These, in truth,
Diverge from one another nowise less
Than."women," vaguely labelled : children some,
With childish voice and nature, lyric bards,
Weaklings that on life's threshold sweetly wail,
But never from that silvery treble pass
Into the note and chant of manliness.
Their love is like their verse, a frail desire,
A fluttering fountain falling feebly back
Into its shallow origin.   Next there are
The poets of contention, wrestlers born,
Who challenge iron Circumstance, and fail :
Generous and strong, withal not strong enough,
Since lacking sinewy wisdom, hard as life.
The love of these is like the lightning spear,
And shrivels whom it touches.   They consume
All things within their reach, and, last of all,
Their lonely selves ; and then through time they tower,
Sublime but charred, and wear on their high fronts
The gloomy glory of the sunlit pine.
But the great gods of Song, in clear white light,
The radiance of their godhead, calmly dwell,
And with immutable cold starlike gaze
Scan both the upper and the under world,
As it revolves, themselves serenely fixed.
Their bias is the bias of the sphere,
That turns all ways, but turns away from none,
Save to return to it.   They have no feud
With gods or men, the living or the dead,
The past or present, and their words complete

Life's incompleteness with a healing note.
For they are not more sensitive than strong,
More wise than tender ; understanding all,
At peace with all, at peace with life and death,
And love that gives a meaning unto life
And takes from death the meaning and the sting :
At peace with hate, and every opposite.
Were I but one of these—presumptuous thought !—
Even you, the live fulfilment of such dreams
As these secrete, would hazard well your love
On my more largely loving.   'Twould be you,
Yes, even you, that first would flag and fail
In either of my choosing ; you, whose wing
Would droop on mine and pray to be upborne.
And when my pinions did no more suffice
For that their double load, then softly down,
Softly and smoothly as descending lark
That hath fulfilled its rhapsody in Heaven,
And with diminished music must decline
To earthy sounds and concepts, I should curb
Illimitable longings to the range
Of lower aspiration.   Were I such !—
But, since I *am* not—

SHE   .

                  Am not ?   Who shall say,
Save she who tests, and haply to her loss ?
'Tis better left untested.   Strange that you,
Who can imagine whatso thing you will,

Should lack imagination to appraise
Imagination at its topmost worth.
Now wield your native sceptre and extend
Your fancy forth where Florence overbrims
In eddies fairer even than herself.
Look how the landscape smiles complacently
At its own beauty, as indeed it may ;
Villa and vineyard each a separate home,
Containing possibilities unseen,
Materials for your pleasure.   Now disport !
Which homestead may it please my lord of song
To chalk for his, as those rough Frenchmen did
Who came with bow-legged Charles to justify
Savonarola's scourgeful prophecies ?
Shall it be that one gazing in our face,
Not jealous of its beauty, but exposed
To all the wantonness of sun and air,
With roses girt, with roses garlanded,
And balustraded terrace topped with jars
Of clove carnations ; unambitious roof,
Italian equivalent to house
Love in a cottage ?   Why, the very place
For her you once described !   Wait !   Let me see,
Can I recall the lines ? Yes, thus they ran.
Do you remember them ?   Or are they now
A chronicle forgotten and erased
From that convenient palimpsest, the heart ?

In dewy covert of her eyes
The secret of the violet lies ;

The sun and wind caress and pair
In the lithe wavelets of her hair ;
The fragrance of the warm soft south
Hovers about her honeyed mouth ;
And, when she moves, she floats through air
Like zepyhr-wafted gossamer.
Hers is no lore of dumb dead books ;
Her learning liveth in her looks ;
And still she shows, in meek replies,
Wisdom enough to deem you wise.
Her voice as soothing is and sweet
As whispers of the waving wheat,
And in the moisture of her kiss   ·
Is April-like deliciousness.
Like gloaming-hour, she doth inspire
A vague, an infinite desire ;
And, like the stars, though out of sight,
Filleth the loneliness of night.
Come how she may, or slow or fleet,
She brings the morning on her feet ;
Gone, leaves behind a nameless pain,
Like the sadness of a silenced strain.

HE

A youthful dream.
  ·

SHE

Yet memory can surmise
That young dream fruited to reality,

Then, like reality, was dream no more.
All dreams are youthful ; you are dreaming still.
What lovely visions denizen your sleep !
Let me recall another ; for I know
All you have written, thought, and felt, and much
You neither thought nor felt, but only sang.
A wondrous gift, a godlike gift, that breathes
Into our exiled clay unexiled lives,
Manlier than Adam, comelier than Eve.
That massive villa, we both know so well,
With one face set toward Settignano, one
Gazing at Bellosguardo, and its rear
Locked from the north by clustered cypresses,
That seem like fixed colossal sentinels,
And tower above its tower, but look not in,
Might be abode for her whom you conceived
In tropes so mystical, you must forgive
If recollection trips.

To dwell with her is calmly to abide
Through every change of time and every flux of tide.

In her the Present, Past, and Future meet,
The Father, and the Son, and dovelike Paraclete.

She holdeth silent intercourse with Night,
Still journeying with the stars, and shining with their
*   light.*

Her love, illumination ; her embrace,
The sweep of angels' wings across a mortal's face.

Her lap is piled with autumn fruits, her brow
Crowned with the blossoming trails that smile from
*   April's bough.*

Like wintry stars that shine with frosty fire,
Her loftiness excites to elevate desire.

To love her is to burn with such a flame
As lights the lamp which bears the Sanctuary's name.

That lamp burns on for ever, day and night,
Before her mystic shrine.   I am its acolyte.

HE

The merest foam of fancy ; foam and spray.

SHE

Foam-drift of fancy that hath ebbed away.
See how the very simile rebukes
Man's all unsealike longings !   For confess,
While ocean still returns, the puny waves
Of mortal love are sucked into the sand,
Their motion felt, their music heard, no more.
Look when the vines are linking hands, and seem
As pausing from the dance of Spring, or just
Preparing to renew it, round and round,
On the green carpet of the bladed corn,
That spreads about their feet : corn, vine, and fig,
Almond and mulberry, cherry, and pear, and peach,

Not taught to know their place, but left to range
Up to the villa's walls, windows, and doors,
And peep into its life and smile good-day,
A portion of its homeliness and joy:
A poet's villa once, a poet's again,
If you but dream it such; a roof for her,
To whom you wrote—I wonder who she was—
This saucy sonnet; saucy, withal sweet,
And O, how true of the reflected love
You poets render to your worshippers.

TRUE AS THE DIAL TO THE SUN

You are the sun, and I the dial, sweet,
So you can mark on me what time you will.
If you move slowly, how can I move fleet?
And, when you halt, I too must fain be still.
Chide not the cloudy humours of my brow,
If you behold no settled sunshine there:
Rather upbraid your own, sweet, and allow,
My looks can not be foul if yours be fair.
Then from the heaven of your high witchery shine,
And I with smiles shall watch the hours glide by;
You have no mood that is not straightway mine;
My cheek but takes complexion from your eye.
All that I am dependeth so on you,
What clouds the sun must cloud the dial too.

HE

No man should quarrel with his Past, and I
Maintain no feud with mine.   Do we not ripen,
Ripen and mellow in love, unto the close,
Thanks no more to the present than the past?
First love is fresh but fugitive as Spring,
A wilding flower no sooner plucked than faded;
And summer's sultry fervour ends in storm,
Recriminating thunder, wasteful tears,
And angry gleam of lightning menaces.
Give me October's meditative haze,
Its gossamer mornings, dewy-wimpled eves,
Dewy and fragrant, fragrant and secure,
The long slow sound of farmward-wending wains,
When homely Love sups quiet 'mong its sheaves,
Sups 'mong its sheaves, its sickle at its side,
And all is peace, peace and plump fruitfulness.

SHE

Picture of all we dream and we desire :
Autumn's grave cheerfulness and sober bliss,
Rich resignation, humble constancy.
For, prone to bear the load piled up by life,
We, once youth's pasture season at an end,
Submit to crawl.   Unbroken to the last,
You spurn the goad of stern taskmaster Time.
Even 'mid autumn harvest you demand
Returning hope and blossom of the Spring,
All seasons and sensations, and at once,

Or in too quick succession.   Do we blame ?
We envy rather the eternal youth
We cannot share.   But youth is pitiless,
And, marching onward, neither asks nor seeks
Who falls behind.   Thus women who are wise,
Beside their thresholds knitting homely gear,
Wave wistful salutation as you pass,
And think of you regretfully, when gone :
A soft regret, a sweet regret, that is
Only the mellow fruit of unplucked joy.
Now improvise some other simple strain,
That with harmonious cadence may attune
The vain and hazard discords of discourse.

HE

When Love was young, it asked for wings,
  That it might still be roaming ;
And away it sped, by fancy led,
  Through dawn, and noon, and gloaming.
Each daintiness that blooms and blows
  It wooed in honeyed metre,
And, when it won the sweetest sweet,
  It flew off to a sweeter :
    When Love was young.

When Love was old, it craved for rest,
  For home, and hearth, and haven ;
For quiet talks round sheltered walks,
  And long lawns smoothly shaven.

And what Love sought, at last it found,
A roof, a porch, a garden,
And, from a fond unquestioning heart,
Peace, sympathy, and pardon,
When Love was old.

SHE

Simple, in sooth, and haply true : withal,
Too, too autumnal even for my heart.
I never weary of your vernal note.
Carol again, and sing me back my youth
With the redundant melodies of Spring.

HE

I breathe my heart in the heart of the rose,
The rose that I pluck and send you,
With a prayer that the perfume its leaves enclose
May kiss, and caress, and tend you :
Caress and tend you till I can come,
To the garden where first I found you,
And the thought that as yet in the rose is dumb
Can ripple in music round you.

O rose, that will shortly be her guest,
You may well look happy, at leaving :
Will you lie in the cradle her snowy breast
Doth rock with its gentle heaving?
Will you mount the throne of her hazel hair,
That waves like a summer billow,

C   N

Or be hidden and hushed, at nightfall prayer,
In the folds of her dimpled pillow ?

And when she awakes at dawn to feel
If you have been dreaming with her,
Then the whole of your secret, sweet rose, reveal,
And say I am coming thither :
And when there is silence in earth and sky,
And peace from the cares that cumber,
She must not ask if your leaves or I
Be clasped in her perfumed slumber.

SHE

Give me your hand ; and, if you will, keep mine
Engraffed in yours, as slowly thus we skirt
La Doccia's dark declivity, and make
Athwart Majano's pathless pines a path
To lead us onward haply where it may.
Lo ! the Carrara mountains flush to view,
That in the noonday were not visible.
Shall we not fold this comfort to our hearts,
Humbly rejoiced to think as there are heights
Seen only in the sunset, so our lives,
If that they lack not loftiness, may wear
A glow of glory on their furrowed fronts,
Until they faint and fade into the night !

AVE MARIA

I

In the ages of Faith, before the day
When men were too proud to weep or pray,
There stood in a red-roofed Breton town
Snugly nestled 'twixt sea and down,
A chapel for simple souls to meet,
Nightly, and sing with voices sweet,

                              Ave Maria !

II

There was an idiot, palsied, bleared,
With unkempt locks and a matted beard,
Hunched from the cradle, vacant-eyed,
And whose head kept rolling from side to side ;
Yet who, when the sunset-glow grew dim,
Joined with the rest in the twilight hymn,

                              Ave Maria !

III

But when they up-got and wended home,
Those up the hillside, these to the foam,

He hobbled along in the narrowing dusk,
Like a thing that is only hull and husk;
On as he hobbled, chanting still,
Now to himself, now loud and shrill,

           Ave Maria !

IV

When morning smiled on the smiling deep,
And the fisherman woke from dreamless sleep,
And ran up his sail, and trimmed his craft,
While his little ones leaped on the sand and laughed,
The senseless cripple would stand and stare,
Then suddenly holloa his wonted prayer,

           Ave Maria !

V

Others might plough, and reap, and sow,
Delve in the sunshine, spin in snow,
Make sweet love in a shelter sweet,
Or trundle their dead in a winding-sheet;
But he, through rapture, and pain, and wrong,
Kept singing his one monotonous song,

           Ave Maria !

VI

When thunder growled from the ravelled wrack,
And ocean to welkin bellowed back,
And the lightning sprang from its cloudy sheath,
And tore through the forest with jaggèd teeth,

Then leaped and laughed o'er the havoc wreaked,
The idiot clapped with his hands, and shrieked,
                              Ave Maria!

VII

Children mocked, and mimicked his feet,
As he slouched or sidled along the street;
Maidens shrank as he passed them by,
And mothers with child eschewed his eye;
And half in pity, half scorn, the folk
Christened him, from the words he spoke,
                              Ave Maria.

VIII

One year when the harvest feasts were done,
And the mending of tattered nets begun,
And the kittiwake's scream took a weirder key
From the wailing wind and the moaning sea,
He was found, at morn, on the fresh-strewn snow,
Frozen, and faint, and crooning low,
                              Ave Maria!

IX

They stirred up the ashes between the dogs,
And warmed his limbs by the blazing logs,
Chafed his puckered and bloodless skin,
And strove to quiet his chattering chin;
But, ebbing with unreturning tide,
He kept on murmuring till he died,
                              Ave Maria!

X

Idiot, soulless, brute from birth,
He could not be buried in sacred earth ;
So they laid him afar, apart, alone,
Without or a cross, or turf, or stone,
Senseless clay unto senseless clay,
To which none ever came nigh to say,

Ave Maria !

XI

When the meads grew saffron, the hawthorn white,
And the lark bore his music out of sight,
And the swallow outraced the racing wave,
Up from the lonely, outcast grave
Sprouted a lily, straight and high,
Such as She bears to whom men cry,

Ave Maria !

XII

None had planted it, no one knew
How it had come there, why it grew ;
Grew up strong, till its stately stem
Was crowned with a snow-white diadem,—
One pure lily, round which, behold !
Was written by God in veins of gold,

" Ave Maria !"

XIII

Over the lily they built a shrine,
Where are mingled the mystic bread and wine ;

Shrine you may see in the little town
That is snugly nestled 'twixt deep and down.
Through the Breton land it hath wondrous fame,
And it bears the unshriven idiot's name,

                        Ave Maria.

XIV

Hunchbacked, gibbering, blear-eyed, halt,
From forehead to footstep one foul fault,
Crazy, contorted, mindless-born,
The gentle's pity, the cruel's scorn,
Who shall bar you the gates of Day,
So you have simple faith to say,

                        Ave Maria?

AGATHA

SHE wanders in the April woods,
　　That glisten with the fallen shower;
She leans her face against the buds,
　　She stops, she stoops, she plucks a flower.
　　She feels the ferment of the hour:
She broodeth when the ringdove broods;
　　The sun and flying clouds have power
Upon her cheek and changing moods.
　　She cannot think she is alone,
　　　　As o'er her senses warmly steal
　　Floods of unrest she fears to own,
　　　　And almost dreads to feel.

Among the summer woodlands wide
　　Anew she roams, no more alone;
The joy she feared is at her side,
　　Spring's blushing secret now is known.
　　The primrose and its mates have flown,

The thrush's ringing note hath died ;
But glancing eye and glowing tone
Fall on her from her god, her guide.
　She knows not, asks not, what the goal,
　　She only feels she moves towards bliss,
　And yields her pure unquestioning soul
　　To touch and fondling kiss.

III

And still she haunts those woodland ways,
　Though all fond fancy finds there now
To mind of spring or summer days,
　Are sodden trunk and songless bough.
　The past sits widowed on her brow :
Homeward she wends with wintry gaze,
　To walls that house a hollow vow,
To hearth where love hath ceased to blaze :
　Watches the clammy twilight wane,
　　With grief too fixed for woe or tear ;
　And, with her forehead 'gainst the pane,
　　Envies the dying year.

A WOMAN'S APOLOGY

In the green darkness of a summer wood,
Wherethro' ran winding ways, a lady stood,
Carved from the air in curving womanhood.

A maiden's form crowned by a matron's mien,
As, about Lammas, wheat-stems may be seen,
The ear all golden, but the stalk still green.

There as she stood, waiting for sight or sound,
Down a dim alley without break or bound,
Slowly he came, his gaze upon the ground.

Nor ever once he lifted up his eyes
Till he no more her presence could disguise;
Then he her face saluted silentwise.

And silentwise no less she turned, as though
She was the leaf and he the current's flow,
And where he went, there she perforce must go.

And both kept speechless as the dumb or dead,
Nor did the earth so much as speak their tread,
So soft by last year's leaves 'twas carpeted.

And not a sound moved all the greenwood through,
Save when some quest with fluttering wings outflew,
Ruffling the leaves ; then silence was anew.

And when the track they followed forked in twain,
They never doubted which one should be ta'en,
But chose as though obeying secret rein.

Until they came where boughs no longer screened
The sky, and soon abruptly intervened
A rustic gate, and over it they leaned.

Leaned over it, and green before them lay
A meadow ribbed with drying swathes of hay,
From which the hinds had lately gone away.

Beyond it, yet more woods, these too at rest,
Smooth-dipping down to shore, unseen, but guessed;
For lo ! the Sea, with nothing on its breast.

I

" I was sure you would come," she said, with a voice like
a broken wing
That flutters, and fails, then flags, while it nurses the
failure's sting ;
" You could not refuse me that, 'tis but such a little thing.

II

"Do I remember the words, the farewell words that you
    spoke,
Answering soft with hard, ere we parted under the oak?
Remember them? Can I forget? For each of them
    cut like a stroke.

III

"True—were they true? You think so, or they had
    never been said;
But somehow, like lightning flashes, they flickered about
    my head,
Flickered but touched me not. They ought to have
    stricken me dead.

IV

"What do I want with you now? What I always
    wanted, you know;
A voice to be heard in the darkness, a flower to be seen
    in the snow,
And a bond linking each fresh future with a lengthening
    long-ago.

V

"Is it too much? Too little! Well, little or much, 'tis
    all
That rescues my life from the nothing it seems to be
    when I call
For a life to reply, and my voice comes back like a voice
    from the wall.

VI

"If one played sweet on a lute, yea so soft that you
 scarce could hear,
Would you clang all the chords with your hand that the
 octaves might ring out clear?
Lo! asunder the strings are snapped, and the music
 shrinks silent for fear.

VII

" See! the earth through the infinite spaces goes silently
 round and round,
And the moon moveth on through the heavens and
 never maketh a sound,
And the wheels of eternity traverse their journey in stillness profound.

VIII

"'Tis only the barren breakers that bellow on barren
 shore;
'Tis only the braggart thunders that rumble and rage and
 roar;
Like a wave is the love that babbles; but silent love
 loves evermore.

IX

" Feeble, shadowy, shallow?   Is ocean then shallow that
 keeps

Its harvest of shell and seaweed that none or garners or
    reaps,
That the diver may sound a moment, but never drag
    from its deeps?

X

"Cowardice? Yes, we are cowards; cowards from
    cradle to bier,
And the terror of life grows upon us as we grow year by
    year;
Our smiles are but trembling ripples urged on by a sub-
    tide of fear.

XI

"And hence, or at substance or shadow we start, though
    we scarce know why.
Life seems like a haunted wood, where we tremble and
    crouch and cry.
Beast, or robber, or ghost,—our courage is still to fly.

XII

"So we look around for a guide, and to place all our
    fears in his hand,
That his courage may keep us brave, that his grandeur
    may make us grand:
But, remember, a guide, not an ambush. Oh, tell me
    you understand!

XIII

"Still silent, still unpersuaded.   Ah! I know what your
    thoughts repeat.
We are all alike, and we love to keep passion aglow at
    our feet,
Like one that sitteth in shade and complacently smiles at
    the heat.

XIV

"You think so?   Then come into shade.   Rise up,
    . take the seat at my side;
Or, see, I will kneel, not you.   What is humble, if this be
    pride?
What seems cold now will chance feel warm when the
    fierce glare of noon hath died.

XV

" Have you never, when waves were breaking, watched
    children at sport on the beach,
With their little feet tempting the foam-fringe, till with
    stronger and further reach
Than they dreamed of, a billow comes bursting, how
    they turn and scamper and screech!

XVI

" Are we more than timider children?   With its blending
    of terror and glee,

To us life—call it love, if you will—is a deep mysterious
    sea,
That we play with till it grows earnest; then straight
    we tremble and flee.

XVII

"Oh, never the pale east flushes with ripples of rising
    day,
Never, never, the birds awakening sing loud upon gable
    and spray,
But afresh you dawn on my life, and my soul chants its
    matin lay.

XVIII

"When the scent of the elder is wafted from the hedge
    in the cottage lane,
Up the walk, and over the terrace, and in at the open
    pane,
You are there, and my life seems perfumed like a garden
    after rain.

XIX

"The nightingale brings you nearer, the woodpecker
    borrows your voice;
The flower where the bees cling and cluster seems the
    flower of the flowers of your choice.
I am sad with the cloud of your sadness, with the joy of
    your joy I rejoice.

xx

"What dearer, what nearer would you? Once heart is
    betrothed to heart,
No closeness can bring them closer, no parting can put
    them apart.
Oh! take all the balm, leave the bitter, give the sweet-
    ness with none of its smart."

The blue sea now had saddened into gray;
Solid and close the darkening woodlands lay,
And twilight's floating dews clung heavy with the hay.

One with all these, he neither stirred nor spake,
Though for a sound the silence seemed to ache,
Waiting and wondering when his voice the pain would
    break.

Then since the words hope forced despair to say
Seemed to have vanished with the vanished day,
She turned her from the gate, and slowly moved away.

And he too turned; but pacing side by side,
This mocking nearness did them more divide,
Than if betwixt them moaned the round of ocean wide.

But when o'erhead boughs once more met and spanned,
She halted, laid upon his arm her hand,
And questioned blank his face, his heart to understand.

Had trust or tenderness been hovering there,
She would have known it in the duskiest air;
But face and form alike of every trace was bare.

Her touch he neither welcomed nor repelled;
Pulses that once had quickened straight seemed quelled;
He stood like one that is by courteous bondage held.

One hand thus foiled, the other rescuing came,
And in the darkness sheltered against shame,
She fawned on him with both, and trembled out his
    name.

Then as a reaper, when the days are meet,
His sickle curves about the bending wheat,
He hollowed out his arms, and harvested his sweet.

XXI

"Now what shall I cling to?" she murmured, "Behold!
    I am weak, you are strong.
Brief, brief is the bridal of summer, the mourning of
    winter is long;
Never leave me unloved to discover love's right was but
    rapturous wrong!"

Again was silence.   Then she slowly felt
The clasp of cruel fondness round her melt,
And heard a voice that seemed the voice of one that
    knelt.

"The long, long mourning of the winter days
Waits sure for them that bask in summer rays;
One must depart, then life is death to one that stays.

"This fixed decree we can nor change nor cheat;
For I must either leave or lose you, sweet,
And all love's triumphs end in death and dark defeat.

"Death is unconscious change, change conscious death.
Better to die outright than gasp for breath.
Life, dead, hath done with pain; Love, lingering,
    suffereth.

"The only loss—and this may you be spared!—
For which who stake on love must be prepared,
Is still that, though life may, yet death can not be
    shared.

" No other pain shall come to you from me.
What love withholds, love needs must ask.   But, see!
Since you embrace love's chains, love's self doth set you
    free."

So free they wandered, drinking with delight
The scented silence of the summer night,
And in the darkness saw what ne'er is seen in light.

Hushed deep in slumber seemed all earthy jars,
And, looking up, they saw, 'twixt leafy bars,
The untrod fields of Heaven glistening with dewy stars.

THE DEATH OF HUSS

In the streets of Constance was heard the shout,
" Masters ! bring the arch-heretic out !"
The stake had been planted, the faggots spread,
And the tongues of the torches flickered red.
" Huss to the flames !" they fiercely cried :
Then the gate of the Convent opened wide.

Into the sun from the dark he came,
His face as fixed as a face in a frame.
His arms were pinioned, but you could see,
By the smile round his mouth, that his soul was free ;
And his eye with a strange bright glow was lit,
Like a star just before the dawn quencheth it.

To the pyre the crowd a pathway made,
And he walked along it with no man's aid ;
Steadily on to the place he trod,
Commending aloud his soul to God.

Aloud he prayed, though they mocked his prayer :
He was the only thing tranquil there.

But, seeing the faggots, he quickened pace,
As we do when we see the loved one's face.
" Now, now, let the torch in the resin flare,
Till my books and body be ashes and air !
But the spirit of both shall return to men,
As dew that rises descends again."

From the back of the crowd where the women wept,
And the children whispered, a peasant stepped.
A goodly faggot was on his back,
Brittle and sere, from last year's stack ;
And he placed it carefully where the torch
Was sure to lick and the flame to scorch.

" Why bring you fresh fuel, friend ? Here are sticks
To burn up a score of heretics."
Answered the peasant, " Because this year,
My hearth will be cold, for is firewood dear ;
And Heaven be witness I pay my toll,
And burn your body to save my soul."

Huss gazed at the peasant, he gazed at the pile,
Then over his features there stole a smile.
" *O Sancta Simplicitas !* By God's troth,
This faggot of yours may save us both,
And He who judgeth perchance prefer
To the victim the executioner !"

Then unto the stake was he tightly tied,
And the torches were lowered and thrust inside.
You could hear the twigs crackle and sputter the flesh,
Then " *Sancta Simplicitas !*" moaned afresh.
'Twas the last men heard of the words he spoke,
Ere to Heaven his soul went up with the smoke.

THE LAST REDOUBT

I

KACELYEVO's slope still felt
The cannon's bolt and the rifles' pelt;
For a last redoubt up the hill remained,
By the Russ yet held, by the Turk not gained.

II

Mehemet Ali stroked his beard;
His lips were clinched and his look was weird;
Round him were ranks of his ragged folk,
Their faces blackened with blood and smoke.

III

"Clear me the Muscovite out!" he cried,
Then the name of "Allah!" resounded wide,
And the rifles were clutched and the bayonets lowered,
And on to the last redoubt they poured.

IV

One fell, and a second quickly stopped
The gap that he left when he reeled and dropped;
The second,—a third straight filled his place;
The third,—and a fourth kept up the race.

V

Many a fez in the mud was crushed,
Many a throat that cheered was hushed,
Many a heart that sought the crest
Found Allah's throne and a houri's breast.

VI

Over their corpses the living sprang,
And the ridge with their musket-rattle rang,
Till the faces that lined the last redoubt
Could see their faces and hear their shout.

VII

In the redoubt a fair form towered,
That cheered up the brave and chid the coward;
Brandishing blade with a gallant air,
His head erect and his temples bare.

VIII

" Fly! they are on us!" his men implored;
But he waved them on with his waving sword.
"It cannot be held; 'tis no shame to go!"
But he stood with his face set hard to the foe.

IX

Then clung they about him, and tugged, and knelt.
He drew a pistol out from his belt,
And fired it blank at the first that set
Foot on the edge of the parapet.

X

Over, that first one toppled; but on
Clambered the rest till their bayonets shone,
As hurriedly fled his men dismayed,
Not a bayonet's length from the length of his blade.

XI

"Yield!" But aloft his steel he flashed,
And down on their steel it ringing clashed;
Then back he reeled with a bladeless hilt,
His honour full, but his life-blood spilt.

XII

Mehemet Ali came and saw
The riddled breast and the tender jaw.
"Make him a bier of your arms," he said,
"And daintily bury this dainty dead!"

XIII

They lifted him up from the dabbled ground;
His limbs were shapely, and soft, and round.
No down on his lip, on his cheek no shade :—
"Bismillah!" they cried, "'tis an Infidel maid!"

XIV

" Dig her a grave where she stood and fell,
'Gainst the jackal's scratch and the vulture's smell.
Did the Muscovite men like their maidens fight,·
In their lines we had scarcely supped to-night."

XV

So a deeper trench 'mong the trenches there
Was dug, for the form as brave as fair ;
And none, till the Judgment trump and shout,
Shall drive her out of the Last Redoubt.

A FARMHOUSE DIRGE

WILL you walk with me to the brow of the hill, to visit
    the farmer's wife,
Whose daughter lies in the churchyard now, eased of the
    ache of life?
Half a mile by the winding lane, another half to the top:
There you may lean o'er the gate and rest; she will want
    me awhile to stop,
Stop and talk of her girl that is gone and no more will
    wake or weep,
Or to listen rather, for sorrow loves to babble its pain to
    sleep.

II

How thick with acorns the ground is strewn, rent from
    their cups and brown!
How the golden leaves of the windless elms come singly
    fluttering down!

The bryony hangs in the thinning hedge, as russet as
harvest corn,
The straggling blackberries glisten jet, the haws are red
on the thorn ;
The clematis smells no more but lifts its gossamer weight
on high ;—
If you only gazed on the year, you would think how
beautiful 'tis to die.

III

The stream scarce flows underneath the bridge ; they
have dropped the sluice of the mill ;
The roach bask deep in the pool above, and the water-
wheel is still.
The meal lies quiet on bin and floor ; and here where
the deep banks wind,
The water-mosses nor sway nor bend, so nothing seems
left behind.
If the wheels of life would but sometimes stop, and the
grinding awhile would cease,
'Twere so sweet to have, without dying quite, just a spell
of autumn peace.

IV

Cottages four, two new, two old, each with its clambering
rose :
Lath and plaster and weather tiles these, brick faced with
stone are those.

Two crouch low from the wind and the rain, and tell of
the humbler days,
Whilst the other pair stand up and stare with a self-
asserting gaze ;
But I warrant you'd find the old as snug as the new did
you lift the latch,
For the human heart keeps no whit more warm under
slate than beneath the thatch.

V

Tenants of two of them work for me, punctual, sober,
true ;
I often wish that I did as well the work I have got
to do.
Think not to pity their lowly lot, nor wish that their
thoughts soared higher ;
The canker comes on the garden rose, and not on the
wilding brier.
Doubt and gloom are not theirs, and so they but work
and love, they live
Rich in the only valid boons that life can withhold or
give.

VI

Here is the railway bridge, and see how straight do the
bright lines keep,
With pheasant copses on either side, or pastures of quiet
sheep.

The big loud city lies far away, far too is the cliff-bound
    shore,
But the trains that travel betwixt them seem as if bur-
    dened with their roar.
Yet, quickly they pass, and leave no trace, not the echo
    e'en of their noise :
Don't you think that silence and stillness are the sweetest
    of all our joys ?

VII

Lo ! yonder the Farm, and these the ruts that the broad-
    wheeled wains have worn,
As they bore up the hill the faggots sere, or the mellow
    shocks of corn.
The hops are gathered, the twisted bines now brown on
    the brown clods lie,
And nothing of all man sowed to reap is seen betwixt
    earth and sky.
Year after year doth the harvest come, though at summer's
    and beauty's cost :
One can only hope, when our lives grow bare, some reap
    what our hearts have lost.

VIII

And this is the orchard, small and rude, and uncared-for,
    but oh ! in spring,
How white is the slope with cherry bloom, and the
    nightingales sit and sing !

You would think that the world had grown young once
　　more, had forgotten death and fear,
That the nearest thing unto woe on earth was the smile
　　of an April tear ;
That goodness and gladness were twin, were one :—The
　　robin is chorister now :
The russet fruit on the ground is piled, and the lichen
　　cleaves to the bough.

IX

Will you lean o'er the gate, whilst I go on? You can
　　watch the farmyard life,
The beeves, the farmer's hope, and the poults, that
　　gladden his thrifty wife ;
Or, turning, look on the hazy weald,—you will not be
　　seen from here,—
Till your thoughts, like it, grow blurred and vague, and
　　mingle the far and near.
Grief is a flood, and not a spring, whatever in grief we
　　say ;
And perhaps her woe, should she see me alone, will run
　　more quickly away.

　　·　　　　·　　　　·　　　　·　　　　·

I

" I thought you would come this morning, ma'am. Yes,
　　Edith at last has gone ;
To-morrow's a week, ay, just as the sun right into her
　　window shone ;

Went with the night, the vicar says, where endeth never
    the day;
But she's left a darkness behind her here I wish she had
    taken away.
She is no longer with us, but we seem to be always with
    her,
In the lonely bed where we laid her last, and can't get
    her to speak or stir.

2

" Yes, I'm at work; 'tis time I was. I should have
    begun before ;
But this is the room where she lay so still, ere they carried
    her past the door.
I thought I never could let her go where it seems so
    lonely of nights ;
But now I am scrubbing and dusting down, and setting
    the place to rights.
All I have kept are the flowers there, the last that stood
    by her bed.
I suppose I must throw them away. *She* looked much
    fairer when she was dead

3

" Thank you, for thinking of her so much. Kind
    thought is the truest friend.   .
I wish you had seen how pleased she was with the
    peaches you used to send.

She tired of *them* too ere the end, so she did with all we
tried;
But she liked to look at them all the same, so we set
them down by her side.
Their bloom and the flush upon her cheek were alike, I
used to say;
Both were so smooth, and soft, and round, and both have
faded away.

4

" I never could tell you how kind too were the ladies up
at the hall;
Every noon, or fair or wet, one of them used to call.
Worry and work seems ours, but yours pleasant and easy
days,
And, when all goes smooth, the rich and poor have
different lives and ways.
Sorrow and death bring men more close, 'tis joy that
puts us apart;
'Tis a comfort to think, though we're severed so, we're
all of us one at heart.

5

"She never wished to be smart and rich, as so many in
these days do,
Nor cared to go in on market days to stare at the gay
and new.

She liked to remain at home and pluck the white violets
    down in the wood ;
She said to her sisters before she died, ' 'Tis so easy to
    be good.'
She must have found it so, I think, and that was the
    reason why
God deemed it needless to leave her here, so took her
    up to the sky.

6

" The vicar says that he knows she is there, and surely
    she ought to be ;
But though I repeat the words, 'tis hard to believe what
    one does not see.
They did not want me to go to the grave, but I could
    not have kept away,
And whatever I do I can only see a coffin and church-
    yard clay.
Yes, I know it's wrong to keep lingering there, and
    wicked and weak to fret ;
And that's why I'm hard at work again, for it helps one
    to forget.

7

" The young ones don't seem to take to work as their
    mothers and fathers did.
We never were asked if we liked or no, but had to obey
    when bid.

There's Bessie won't swill the dairy now, nor Richard
    call home the cows,
And all of them cry, 'How *can* you, mother?' when I
    carry the wash to the sows.
Edith would help me to clean the pans, to burnish the
    grate and hobs;
But she was so pretty I could not bear to set her on
    dirty jobs.

8

"I don't know how it'll be with them when sorrow and
    loss are theirs,
For it isn't likely that they'll escape their pack of worrits
    and cares.
They say it's an age of progress this, and a sight of
    things improves,
But sickness, and age, and bereavement seem to work in
    the same old grooves.
Fine they may grow, and that, but Death as lief takes
    the moth as the grub.
When their dear ones die, I suspect they'll wish they'd a
    floor of their own to scrub.

9

"Some day they'll have a home of their own, much
    grander than this, no doubt,
But polish the porch as you will you can't keep doctors
    and coffins out.

I've done very well with my fowls this year, but what are
  pullets and eggs,
When the heart in vain at the door of the grave the
  return of the lost one begs?
The rich have leisure to wail and weep, the poor haven't
  time to be sad:
If the cream hadn't been so contrairy this week, I think
  grief would have driven me mad.

10

" How does my husband bear up, you ask?   Well, thank
  you, ma'am, fairly well ;
For he too is busy just now, you see, with the wheat and
  the hops to sell :
It's when the work of the day is done, and he comes
  indoors at night,
While the twilight hangs round the window-panes before
  I bring in the light,
And takes down his pipe, and says not a word, but
  watches the faggots roar—
And then I know he is thinking of her who will sit on
  his knee no more.

11

" Must you be going?   It seems so short.   But thank
  you for thinking to come ;
It does me good to talk of it all, and grief feels doubled
  when dumb.

And the butter's not quite so good this week, if you please,
    ma'am, you must not mind,
And I'll not forget to send the ducks and all the eggs we
    can find ;
I've scarcely had time to look round me yet, work gets
    into such arrears,
With only one pair of hands, and those fast wiping away
    one's tears.

12

"You've got some flowers, yet, haven't you, ma'am?
    though they now must be going fast ;
We never have any to speak of here, and I placed on her
    coffin the last.
Could you spare me a few for Sunday next?   I should
    like to go all alone,
And lay them down on the little mound where there
    isn't as yet a stone.
Thank you kindly, I'm sure they'll do, and I promise to
    heed what you say ;
I'll only just go and lay them there, and then I will come
    away."

X

Come, let us go.   Yes, down the hill, and home by the
    winding lane.
The low-lying fields are suffused with haze, as life is
    suffused with pain.

The noon mists gain on the morning sun, so despondency
　　gains on youth ;
We grope, and wrangle, and boast, but Death is the only
　　certain truth.
O love of life ! what a foolish love ! we should weary of
　　life did it last.
While it lingers, it is but a little thing ; 'tis nothing at all
　　when past.

XI

The acorns thicker and thicker lie, the bryony limper
　　grows,
There are mildewing beads on the leafless brier where
　　once smiled the sweet dog-rose.
You may see the leaves of the primrose push through the
　　litter of sodden ground ;
Their pale stars dream in the wintry womb, and the
　　pimpernel sleepeth sound.
They will awake ; shall *we* awake ?　Are we more than
　　imprisoned breath ?
When the heart grows weak, then hope grows strong, but
　　stronger than hope is Death.

OUTSIDE THE VILLAGE CHURCH

I

" THE old Church doors stand open wide,
    Though neither bells nor anthems peal.
Gazing so fondly from outside,
    Why do you enter not and kneel?

II

" It is the sunset hour when all
    Begin to feel the need to pray,
Upon our common Father call
    To guard the night, condone the day.

III

" Is it proud scorn, or humble doubt,
    That keeps you standing, lingering, there ;
Half in the Church, and half without,
    Midway betwixt the world and prayer?

IV

" No meeter moment could there be
  For man to talk alone with God.
The careless sexton has, you see,
  Shouldered his spade, and homeward trod.

V

" The Vicar's daily round is done ;
  His back just sank below the brow.
He passed the porches, one by one,
  That line the hamlet street, and now

VI

' " He, in his garden, cons the page,
  And muses on to-morrow's text.
The homebound rustic counts his wage,
  The same last week, the same the next.

VII

" Nor priest nor hind are you, but each
  Alike is welcome here within ;
Both they who learn, and they who teach,
  Have secret sorrow, secret sin.

VIII

" Enter, and bare your inmost sore ;
  Enter, and weep your stain away ;
Leave doubt and darkness at the door ;
  Come in and kneel, come in and pray."

IX

Such were the words I seemed to hear,
  By no one uttered, but alack !
The voice of many a bygone year,
  Striking the church, and echoing back.

X

I entered not, but on a stone
  Sate, that recorded some one's loss ;
But name and date no more were shown,
  · The deep-cut lines were smooth with moss.

XI

Below were longsome tags of rhyme,
  But what, you could not now surmise.
Alas ! alas ! that death and time
  Should overgrow love's eulogies.

XII

Round me was Death that plainly spoke
  The hopes and aims that life denied ;
The curious pomp of simple folk,
  The pedantry of rustic pride.

XIII

Some slept in square sepulchral caves,
  Some were stretched flat, and some inurned ;
And there were fresh brown baby graves,
  Resembling cradles overturned.

XIV

From where I sate I still could watch
　The old oak pews, the altar white.
Gable and oasthouse, tile and thatch,
　Smiled softly in the sunset light.

XV

From here and there a cottage roof,
　Spires of blue vapour 'gan to steal ;
To eyes of love a heavenly proof
　The mother warmed the evening meal.

XVI

No more the mill-stream chafed and churned ;
　The wheel hung still, the meal lay whole ;
From marsh and dyke the rooks returned,
　And circled round and round the toll.

XVII

The lambs were mute, the sheep were couched,
　The hop-poles bent 'neath leaf and bine ;
Adown the road the vagrant slouched,
　And glanced up at the alehouse sign.

XVIII

Again I heard the unseen voice :
　"Why do you come not in and rest ?
Whether you grieve or you rejoice,
　You here will be a welcome guest.

XIX

" To Heaven it is the half-way house,
Where hope can feed, and anguish may
Recline its limbs and rest its brows,
With simple thanks for ample pay.

XX

" Was it not here you got the name
Which is of you so close a part,
That, uttered, it hath magic claim
To flush love's cheek, to flood love's heart ?

XXI

" Here too it was, when youth confessed
The weariness of random ways,
And felt a surging in the breast
For faithful nights and fruitful days,

XXII

" You came with one who, conquering fear
When love surprised first thought to fly,
Acknowledged with a tender tear
The sweetness of captivity.

XXIII

" And here 'twill be when you have ta'en
Last look of love, last look of Spring,
When hearts for you will yearn in vain,
And vain for you the birds will sing,.

XXIV

" That shuffling feet and slow will come,
    With cumbrous coffin, gloomy pall,
And, while within you moulder dumb,
    That prayers will rise and tears will fall.

XXV

" And should Death haply prove your friend,
    And what in life was scorned should save,
Hither it is that feet will wend,
    To read the name upon your grave."

XXVI

I heard the voice no more.   The rooks
    Had ceased to float, had ceased to caw ;
The sunlight lingered but in nooks,
    And, gazing toward the west, I saw,

XXVII

Beyond the pasture's withered bents,
    Upstanding hop, recumbent fleece,
And sheaves of wheat, like weathered tents,
    A twilight bivouac of peace.

XXVIII

Into itself the voice withdrew.
    A something subtle all around
Came floating on the rising dew,
    And sweetness took the place of sound.

XXIX

No word of mine, although my heart
    Rebelled, the scented stillness shook ;
But silence seemed to take my part,
    Thus mildly answering mild rebuke :

XXX

" 'Tis true I have to you not brought
    My eager or despondent mood,
But still by wood and stream have sought
    The sanctity of solitude.

XXXI

" But as a youth who quits his home
    To range in tracts of freër fame,
However far or wide he roam,
    Dwells fondly on his mother's name ;

XXXII

" So bear me witness, dear old Church,
    Although apart our ritual be,
I ne'er have breathed one word to smirch
    The Creed that bore and suckled me.

XXXIII

" Not mine presumptuous thought to cope
    With sage's faith, with saint's belief,
Or proudly mock the humble hope
    That solaced the Repentant Thief.

XXXIV

"I do not let the elms, that shut
  My garden in from world without,
Exclude your sacred presence, but
  I lop them when they shoot and sprout;

XXXV

"That I at eve, that I at dawn,
  That I, when noons are warm and still,
Lying or lingering on the lawn,
  May see your tower upon the hill.

XXXVI

"But when Faith grows a sophist's theme,
  And chancels ring with doubt and din,
I sometimes think that they who seem
  The most without, are most within.

XXXVII

"The name you gave, that name I bear;
  The bond you sealed, I sacred keep;
And, when my brain is dust and air,
  Let me within your precincts sleep."

XXXVIII

The sexton came and scanned once more
  The neat square pit of smooth blue clay,
Then turned the key and locked the door,
  And so, like him, I went my way.

XXXIX

I had the summons not obeyed ;
    I had nor knelt nor uttered word ;
But somehow felt that I had prayed,
    And somehow felt I had been heard.

AT SAN GIOVANNI DEL LAGO

I

I LEANED upon the rustic bridge,
　And watched the streamlet make
Its chattering way past zigzag ridge
　Down to the silent lake.

II

The sunlight flickered on the wave,
　Lay quiet on the hill;
Italian sunshine, bright and brave,
　Though 'twas but April still.

III

I heard the distant shepherd's shout,
　I heard the fisher's call;
The lizards glistened in and out,
　Along the crannied wall.

IV

Hard-by, in rudely frescoed niche,
　Hung Christ upon the tree;
Round Him the Maries knelt, and each
　Was weeping bitterly.

V

A nightingale from out the trees
　Rippled, and then was dumb;
But in the golden bays the bees
　Kept up a constant hum.

VI

Two peasant women of the land,
　Barefoot, with tresses black,
Came slowly toward me from the strand,
　With their burdens on their back:

VII

Two wicker crates with linen piled,
　Just newly washed and wrung;
And, close behind, a little child
　That made the morning young.

VIII

Reaching the bridge, each doffed her load,
　Resting before they clomb,
Along the stony twisting road,
　Up to their mountain home.

F　　　　　　　　　　　　　　　　N

IX

Shortly the child, just half its height,
  Stooped 'neath her mother's pack,
And strove and strove with all her might
  To lift it on her back.

X

Thereat my heart began to smile :
  Haply I speak their tongue :
" Can you," I said, " not wait awhile ?
  You won't be always young.

XI

" Why long to share the toil you see,
  Why hurry on the years,
When life will one long season be
  Of labour and of tears ?

XII

" Be patient with your childhood.   Work
  Will come full soon enough.
From year to year, from morn till murk,
  Life will be hard and rough.

XIII

" And yours will grow, and haply I,
  Revisiting this shore,
In years to come will see and sigh
  You are a child no more.

XIV

"Yours then will be the moil, the heat,
  Yours be the strain and stress.
Pray Heaven Love then attend your feet
  To make life's burden less."

XV

Thus as I spoke, with steadfast stare
  She clung between the two,
Scarce understanding, yet aware
  That the sad words were true.

XVI

Down from the mother's face a tear
  Fell to her naked feet.
"But now unto the Signor, dear,
  Your poesy repeat."

XVII

Without demur the little maid
  Spread out her palms, and lo!
From lips that lisped, yet unafraid,
  Sweet verse began to flow.

XVIII

She told the story that we all
  Learn at our mother's knee,
Of Eve's transgression, Adam's fall,
  And Heaven's great clemency:

XIX

How Jesus was by Mary's hands
    In the rough manger laid,
And by rich Kings from far-off lands
    Was pious homage paid :

XX

Then how, though cruel Herod slew
    The suckling babes, and thought
To baffle God, Christ lived and grew,
    And in the temple taught. ˙

XXI

She raised her hands to suit the rhyme,
    She clasped them on her heart ;
There never lived the city mime
    So well had played the part.

XXII

When she broke off, I was too choked
    With tenderness to speak.
And so her little form I stroked,
    And kissed her on the cheek ;

XXIII

And took a sweetmeat that I had,
    And put it in her mouth.
O then she danced like a stream that's glad
    When it hurries to the south.

XXIV

She danced, she skipped, she kissed "good-bye,"
  She frolicked round and round :
The pair resumed their packs, and I
  Sate rooted to the ground.

XXV

" *A rivederla !*"   Then the three
  Went winding up the hill.
Ah ! they have long forgotten me ;
  But I remember still.

BELLAGIO.

THE LAST NIGHT

I

SISTER, come to the chestnut toll,
And sit with me on the dear old bole,
Where we oft have sate in the sun and the rain
And perhaps I never shall sit again.
Longer and darker the shadows grow:
'Tis my last night, dear. With the dawn I go.

II

O the times, and times, we two have played
Alone, alone, in its nursing shade.
When once we the breadth of the park had crossed,
We fancied ourselves to be hid and lost
In a secret world that seemed to be
As vast as the forests I soon shall see.

III

Do you remember the winter days
When we piled up the leaves and made them blaze,
While the blue smoke curled, in the frosty air,
Up the great wan trunks that rose gaunt and bare,
And we clapped our hands, and the rotten bough
Came crackling down to our feet, as now?

IV

But dearer than all was the April weather,
When off we set to the woods together,
And piled up the lap of your clean white frock
With primrose, and bluebell, and ladysmock,
And notched the pith of the sycamore stem
Into whistles. Do you remember them?

V

And in summer you followed me fast and far—
How cruel and selfish brothers are!—
With tottering legs and with cheeks aflame,
Till back to the chestnut toll we came,
And rested and watched the long tassels swing,
That seemed with their scent to prolong the Spring.

VI

And in autumn 'twas still our favourite spot,
When school was over and tasks forgot,
And we scampered away and searched till dusk
For the smooth bright nuts in the prickly husk,
And carried them home, by the shepherd's star,
Then roasted them on the nursery bar.

VII

O, Winnie, I do not want to go
From the dear old home; I love it so.
Why should I follow the sad sea-mew
To a land where everything is new,
Where we never bird-nested, you and I,
Where I was not born, but perhaps shall die?

VIII

No, I did not mean that. ·Come, dry your tears.
You may want them all in the coming years.
There's nothing to cry for, Win : be brave.
I will work like a horse, like a dog, like a slave,
And will come back long ere we both are old,
The clods of my clearing turned to gold.

IX

But could I not stay and work at home,
Clear English woods, turn up English loam ?
I shall have to work with my hands out there,
Shear sheep, shoe horses, put edge on share,
Dress scab, drive bullocks, trim hedge, clean ditch,
Put in here a rivet and there a stitch.

X

It were sweeter to moil in the dear old land,
And sooth why not ?   Have we grown so grand ?
So grand !   When the rear becomes the van,
Rich idleness makes the gentleman.
Gentleman !   What is a gentleman now ?
A swordless hand and a helmless brow.

XI

Would you blush for me, Win, if you saw me there
With my sleeves turned up and my sinews bare,
And the axe on the log come ringing down
Like a battering-ram on a high-walled town,
And my temples beaded with diamond sweat,
As bright as a wealth-earned coronet ?

XII

And, pray, if not there, why here? Does crime
Depend upon distance, or shame on clime?
Will your sleek-skinned plutocrats cease to scoff
At a workman's hands, if he works far off?
And is theirs the conscience men born to sway
Must accept for their own in this latter day?

XIII

I could be Harry's woodreeve. Who should scorn
To work for his House, and the eldest-born?
I know every trunk, and bough, and stick,
Much better than Glebe and as well as Dick.
Loving service seems banned in a monied age,
Or a brother's trust might be all my wage.

XIV

Or his keeper, Win? Do you think I'd mind
Being out in all weathers, wet, frost, or wind?
Because I have got a finer coat,
Do I shrink from a weasel or dread a stoat?
Have I not nailed them by tens and scores
To the pheasant-hutch and the granary doors?

XV

Don't I know where the partridge love to hatch,
And wouldn't the poachers meet their match?
A hearty word has a wondrous charm,
And, if not—well, there's always the stalwart arm.
Thank Heaven! spite pillows and counterpanes,
The blood of the savage still haunts my veins.

XVI

They may boast as they will of our moral days,
Our mincing manners and softer ways,
And our money value for everything.
But he who will fight should alone be King ;
And when gentlemen go, unless I'm wrong,
Men too will grow scarce before very long.

XVII

There, enough ! let us back.   I'm a fool, I know ;
But I *must* see Gladys before I go.
Good-bye, old toll.   In my log-hut bleak,
I shall hear your leaves whisper, your branches creak,
Your woodquests brood, your woodpeckers call,
And the shells of your ripened chestnuts fall.

XVIII

Harry never must let the dear old place
To a stranger's foot and a stranger's face.
He may live as our fathers lived before,
With a homely table and open door.
But out on the pomp the upstart hires,
And that drives a man from the roof of his sires !

XIX

I never can understand why they
Who founded thrones in a braver day,
Should cope with the heroes of 'change and mart
Whose splendour puts rulers and ruled apart,
Insults the lowly and saps the State,
Makes the servile cringe, and the manly hate.

XX

You will write to me often, dear, when I'm gone,
And tell me how everything goes on ;
If the trout spawn well, where the beagles meet,
Who is married or dies in the village street ;
And mind you send me the likeliest pup
Of Fan's next litter.   There, Win, cheer up !

NATURE AND THE BOOK

I

I CLOSED the book. The summer shower
    In smiling dimples ebbed away,
But still on leaf, and blade, and flower,
    The fallen raindrops glistening lay.

II

I placed the volume on the shelf,
    And, issuing from the leafy shed,
Paced the moist garden by myself,
    Musing on what I just had read:

III

That Man should live by Nature's laws,
    And that his ways are waste and wild,
Unless he follow where she draws,
    Cling to her skirts, and be her child:

IV

That love, and dread, and doubt are dreams,
  But dwindling specks in widening space,
Nor shall we ever pierce what seems,
  Or find a soul behind the face ;

V

That if man will but ask the air,
  Question the earth, consult the skies,
He needs no help of awe or prayer,
  Or further wisdom, to be wise.

VI

The sun had dried the garden seat ;
  The tall lithe flax nor bent nor swayed ;
The tassels of the lime smelt sweet
  Within the circle of its shade.

VII

The heavy bees from out the hive
  Came slowly answering to the sun ;
I watched them hover, and then dive
  Into the foxgloves, one by one.

VIII

Shortly a butcher-bird shot by,
  Then doubled back, and upward flew,
Chasing a sulphur butterfly
  To whom the earth and air were new.

IX

Oft it escaped—escaped again,—
    But, each time, feebler swerved and rose ;
Till flagged the flying flower, and then
    I saw not, but could guess, the close.

X

Anon a hawk, intent to strike,
    In the blue ether hovering brown,
Flickered an instant, and, then like
    Returning arrow, quickened down.

XI

What ! Has he missed ? No, bravely done !
    A whirr of wings, a silenced shriek.
Off skimmed the covey—all save one,
    Left in tight claw and rending beak.

XII

And are these then the laws that I
    Must copy with a docile will ?
Am I to suck each sweetness dry ?
    Am I to harry and to kill ?

XIII

If Nature is to be my guide,
    I doubt her fitness for the part,
Rebuke her ruthlessness, and chide
    Her lack of soul, her want of heart.

XIV

I chafe within the cage of law;
  The realm of chance far sweeter is.
I own no love, I feel no awe,
  For causes and for sequences.

XV

Doth Nature draw me, 'tis because,
  Unto my seeming, there doth lurk
A lawlessness about her laws,   .
  More mood than purpose in her work.

XVI

The Spring-time will not come to date;
  Winds, clouds, and frosts, man's reckoning mar.
For bud and bloom you have to wait,
  Despite your ordered calendar.

XVII

If Nature built by rule and square,
  Than man what wiser would she be?
What wins us is her careless care,
  And sweet unpunctuality.

XVIII

They misconstrue her, who translate,
  They blur her mirror with their mist.
" Behold," one says, " the face of Fate,"
  Because himself a fatalist.

XIX

Another, coming, cries "Behold
The aspect of a veering will !
The Gods are weak, the Gods are old "—
Fools ! you are older, weaker still.

XX

In vain would science scan and trace
Firmly her aspect.   All the while,
There gleams upon her far-off face
A vague unfathomable smile.

XXI

Only the poet reads her right,
Because he reads with heart, not eyes :
He bares his being in her sight,
And mirrors all her mysteries.

XXII

While others scan some favourite part
Of Nature, he reflects the whole,
Has every climate in his heart,
And all the seasons in his soul.

XXIII

While she upon herself revolves,
He only her whole sphere can see,
And in that prism, his mind, resolves
The fragments of her unity.

XXIV

He bids her not to him conform,
  He does not question her intent ;
He takes the sunshine and the storm
  As strings of some sweet instrument ;

XXV

And out of these, and every mood
  That in her lurks, makes music flow,
And fledges Fancy's happy brood
  E'en from the very nest of woe.

XXVI

He loves her, hence doth not demand
  That she be better or be worse,
But links with his her helpful hand,
  And weds her beauty to his verse.

XXVII

He loves her more, as grow the years ;
  Her faults are virtues in his eyes ;
He drinks, with her, Spring's wayward tears,
  With her, shares Winter's wasted sighs.

XXVIII

She waited for him till he came ;
  Though he departs, she doth survive,
And, fondly careful of his fame,
  Through hers she keeps his name alive.

G   N

XXIX

From sunny woof and cloudy weft
Fell rain in sheets ; so, to myself
I hummed these hazard rhymes, and left
The learnèd volume on the shelf.

GRANDMOTHER'S TEACHING

I

"GRANDMOTHER dear, you do not know; you have lived
    the old-world life,
Under the twittering eave of home, sheltered from storm
    and strife;
Rocking cradles, and covering jams, knitting socks for
    baby feet,
Or piecing together lavender bags for keeping the linen
    sweet:
Daughter, wife, and mother in turn, and each with a blame-
    less breast,
Then saying your prayers when the nightfall came, and
    quietly dropping to rest.

II

"You must not think, Granny, I speak in scorn, for yours
    have been well-spent days,
And none ever paced with more faithful feet the dutiful
    ancient ways.
Grandfather's gone, but while he lived you clung to him
    close and true,

And mother's heart, like her eyes, I know, came to her
    straight from you.
If the good old times, at the good old pace, in the good
    old grooves would run,
One could not do better, I'm sure of that, than do as
    you all have done.

III

"But the world has wondrously changed, Granny, since
    the days when you were young ;
It thinks quite different thoughts from then, and speaks
    with a different tongue.
The fences are broken, the cords are snapped, that
    tethered man's heart to home ;
He ranges free as the wind or the wave, and changes his
    shore like the foam.
He drives his furrows through fallow seas, he reaps what
    the breakers sow,
And the flash of his iron flail is seen 'mid the barns of
    the barren snow.

IV

"He has lassoed the lightning and led it home, he has
    yoked it unto his need,
And made it answer the rein and trudge as straight as
    the steer or steed.
He has bridled the torrents and made them tame, he has
    bitted the champing tide,
It toils as his drudge and turns the wheels that spin for
    his use and pride.

He handles the planets and weighs their dust, he mounts
    on the comet's car,
And he lifts the veil of the sun, and stares in the eyes of
    the uttermost star.

V

" 'Tis not the same world you knew, Granny ; its fetters
    have fallen off ;
The lowliest now may rise and rule where the proud used
    to sit and scoff.
No need to boast of a scutcheoned stock, claim rights
    from an ancient wrong ;
All are born with a silver spoon in their mouths whose
    gums are sound and strong.
And I mean to be rich and great, Granny ; I mean it
    with heart and soul :
At my feet is the ball, I will roll it on, till it spins through
    the golden goal.

VI

" Out on the thought that my copious life should trickle
    through trivial days,
Myself but a lonelier sort of beast, watching the cattle
    graze,
Scanning the year's monotonous change, gaping at wind
    and rain,
Or hanging with meek solicitous eyes on the whims of a
    creaking vane ;

Wretched if ewes drop single lambs, blest so is oilcake
 cheap,
And growing old in a tedious round of worry, surfeit, and
 sleep.

VII

"You dear old Granny, how sweet your smile, and how
 soft your silvery hair!
But all has moved on while you sate still in your cap and
 easy-chair.
The torch of knowledge is lit for all, it flashes from hand
 to hand;
The alien tongues of the earth converse, and whisper
 from strand to strand.
The very churches are changed and boast new hymns,
 new rites, new truth;
Men worship a wiser and greater God than the half-
 known God of your youth.

VIII

"What! marry Connie and set up house, and dwell
 where my fathers dwelt,
Giving the homely feasts they gave and kneeling where
 they knelt?
She is pretty, and good, and void I am sure of vanity,
 greed, or guile;
But she has not travelled nor seen the world, and is
 lacking in air and style.

Women now are as wise and strong as men, and vie with
  men in renown;
The wife that will help to build my fame was not bred
  near a country town.

IX

" What a notion ! to figure at parish boards, and wrangle
  o'er cess and rate,
I, who mean to sit for the county yet, and vote on an
  Empire's fate;
To take the chair at the Farmers' Feast, and tickle their
  bumpkin ears,
Who must shake a senate before I die, and waken a
  people's cheers !
In the olden days was no choice, so sons to the roof of
  their fathers clave :
But now ! 'twere to perish before one's time, and to sleep
  in a living grave.

X

" I see that you do not understand.   How should you ?
  Your memory clings
To the simple music of silenced 'days and the skirts of
  vanishing things.
Your fancy wanders round ruined haunts, and dwells
  upon oft-told tales ;
Your eyes discern not the widening dawn, nor your ears
  catch the rising gales.

But live on, Granny, till I come back, and then perhaps
    you will own
The dear old Past is an empty nest, and the Present the
    brood that is flown."

I

" And so, my dear, you've come back at last? I always
    fancied you would.
Well, you see the old home of your childhood's days is
    standing where it stood.
The roses still clamber from porch to roof, the elder is
    white at the gate,
And over the long smooth gravel path the peacock still
    struts in state.
On the gabled lodge, as of old, in the sun, the pigeons
    sit and coo,
And our hearts, my dear, are no whit more changed, but
    have kept still warm for you.

II

" You'll find little altered, unless it be me, and that since
    my last attack ;
But so that you only give me time, I can walk to the
    church and back.
You bade me not die till you returned, and so you see
    I lived on :
I'm glad that I did now you've really come, but it's
    almost time I was gone.

I suppose that there isn't room for us all, and the old
    should depart the first.
That's as it should be. What is sad, is to bury the
    dead you've nursed.

III

"Won't you have bit nor sup, my dear? Not even a
    glass of whey?
The dappled Alderney calved last week, and the baking
    is fresh to-day.
Have you lost your appetite too in town, or is it you've
    grown over-nice?
If you'd rather have biscuits and cowslip wine, they'll
    bring them up in a trice.
But what am I saying? Your coming down has set me
    all in a maze :
I forgot that you travelled here by train; I was thinking
    of coaching days.

IV

"There, sit you down, and give me your hand, and tell
    me about it all,
From the day that you left us, keen to go, to the pride
    that had a fall.
And all went well at the first? So it does, when we're
    young and puffed with hope ;
But the foot of the hill is quicker reached the easier
    seems the slope.

And men thronged round you, and women too! Yes,
    that I can understand.
When there's gold in the palm, the greedy world is eager
    to grasp the hand.

V

"I heard them tell of your smart town house, but I
    always shook my head.
One doesn't grow rich in a year and a day, in the time
    of my youth 'twas said.
Men do not reap in the spring, my dear, nor are granaries
    filled in May,
Save it be with the harvest of former years, stored up for
    a rainy day.
The seasons will keep their own true time, you can hurry
    nor furrow nor sod:
It's honest labour and steadfast thrift that alone are blest
    by God.

VI

"You say you were honest. I trust you were, nor do I
    judge you, my dear:
I have old-fashioned ways, and it's quite enough to keep
    one's own conscience clear.
But still the commandment, "Thou shalt not steal,"
    though a simple and ancient rule,
Was not made for modern cunning to baulk, nor for any
    new age to befool;

And if my growing rich unto others brought but penury,
 chill, and grief,
I should feel, though I never had filched with my hands,
 I was only a craftier thief.

VII

"That isn't the way they look at it there? All wor-
 shipped the rising sun?
Most of all the fine lady, in pride of purse you fancied
 your heart had won.
I don't want to hear of her beauty or birth: I reckon
 her foul and low;
Far better a steadfast cottage wench than grand loves
 that come and go.
To cleave to their husbands, through weal, through woe,
 is all women have to do:
In growing as clever as men they seem to have matched
 them in fickleness too.

VIII

"But there's one in whose heart has your image still
 dwelt through many an absent day,
As the scent of a flower will haunt a closed room,
 though the flower be taken away.
Connie's not quite so young as she was, no doubt, but
 faithfulness never grows old;
And were beauty the only fuel of love, the warmest
 hearth soon would grow cold.

Once you thought that she had not travelled, and knew
    neither the world nor life :
Not to roam, but to deem her own hearth the whole
    world, that's what a man wants in a wife.

IX

" I'm sure you'd be happy with Connie, at least if your
    own heart's in the right place.
She will bring you nor power, nor station, nor wealth,
    but she never will bring you disgrace.
They say that the moon, though she moves round the
    earth, never turns to him morning or night
But one face of her sphere, and it must be because she's
    so true a satellite ;
And Connie, if into your orbit once drawn by the sacra-
    ment sanctioned above,
Would revolve round you constantly, only to show the
    one-sided aspect of love.

X

" You will never grow rich by the land, I own ; but if
    Connie and you should wed,
It will feed your children and household too, as it you
    and your fathers fed.
The seasons have been unkindly of late ; there's a
    wonderful cut of hay,
But the showers have washed all the goodness out, till
    it's scarcely worth carting away.

There's a fairish promise of barley straw, but the ears
  look rusty and slim :
I suppose God intends to remind us thus that something depends on Him.

XI

"God neither progresses nor changes, dear, as I once
  heard you rashly say :
Man's schools and philosophies come and go, but His
  word doth not pass away.
We worship Him here as we did of old, with simple and
  reverent rite :
In the morning we pray Him to bless our work, to
  forgive our transgressions at night.
To keep His commandments, to fear His name, and
  what should be done, to do,—
That's the beginning of wisdom still; I suspect 'tis the
  end of it too.

XII

"You must see the new-fangled machines at work, that
  harrow, and thresh, and reap ;
They're wonderful quick, there's no mistake, and they
  say in the end they're cheap.
But they make such a clatter, and seem to bring the rule
  of the town to the fields :
There's something more precious in country life than the
  balance of wealth it yields.

But that seems going; I'm sure I hope that I shall be
  gone before :
Better poor sweet silence of rural toil than the factory's
  opulent roar.

XIII

" They're a mighty saving of labour, though ; so at least
  I hear them tell,
Making fewer hands and fewer mouths, but fewer hearts
  as well :
They sweep up so close that there's nothing left for
  widows and bairns to glean ;
If machines are growing like men, man seems to be
  growing a half machine.
There's no friendliness left ; the only tie is the wage upon
  Saturday nights :
Right used to mean duty ; you'll find that now there's no
  duty, but only rights.

XIV

" Still stick to your duty, my dear, and then things cannot
  go much amiss.
What made folks happy in bygone times, will make them
  happy in this.
There's little that's called amusement, here ; but why
  should the old joys pall ?
Has the blackbird ceased to sing loud in spring ? Has
  the cuckoo forgotten to call ?

Are bleating voices no longer heard when the cherry-
blossoms swarm?
And have home, and children, and fireside lost one
gleam of their ancient charm?

XV

" Come, let us go round; to the farmyard first, with its
litter of fresh-strewn straw,
Past the ash-tree dell, round whose branching tops the
young rooks wheel and caw;
Through the ten-acre mead that was mown the first, and
looks well for aftermath,
Then round by the beans—I shall tire by then,—and
home up the garden-path,
Where the peonies hang their blushing heads, where the
larkspur laughs from its stalk—
With my stick and your arm I can manage.   But see!
There, Connie comes up the walk."

TWO VISIONS

WRITTEN, 1863.   REVISED, 1889

I

THE curtains of the night were folded
  Round sleep-entangled sense ;
So that the things I saw were moulded,
  I know not how, nor whence.

II

But I beheld a smokeless city,
  Built upon jutting slopes,
Up whose steep paths, as if for pity,
  Stretched loosely-hanging ropes.

III

Withal, of many who ascended,
  No one appeared to use
This aid, allowed in days since mended,
  When folks had weaker thews.

IV

The men, still animal in vigour,
Strode stalwart and erect;
But on their brows, in placid rigour,
Reigned sovereign Intellect.

V

Women round-limbed, sound-lunged, full-breasted,
Walked at a rhythmic pace;
Yet not the less, for that, invested
With every female grace.

VI

Fearless, unveiled, and unattended,
Strolled maidens to and fro :
Youths looked respect, but never bended
Obsequiously low.

VII

And each with other, sans condition,
Held parley brief or long,
Without provoking coarse suspicion
Of marriage, or of wrong.

VIII

All were well clad, but none were better,
And gems beheld I none,
Save where there hung a jewelled fetter,
Symbolic, in the sun.

H

IX

I saw a noble-looking maiden
　Close Dante's solemn book,
And go, with crate of linen laden,
　And wash it in the brook.

X

Anon, a broad-browed poet, dragging
　A load of logs along,
To warm his hearth, withal not flagging
　In current of his song.

XI'

Each one some handicraft attempted,
　Or helped to till the soil :
None but the agëd were exempted
　From communistic toil :

XII

Which was nor long nor unremitting,
　Since shared in by the whole ;
Leaving to each one, as is fitting,
　Full leisure for the Soul.

XIII

Was many a group in allocution
　On problems that delight,
And lift, when e'en beyond solution,
　Man to a nobler height.

XIV

And oftentimes was brave contention,
    Such as beseems the wise ;
But always courteous abstention
    From over-swift replies.

XV

Age lorded not, nor rose the hectic
    Up to the cheek of Youth ;
But reigned throughout their dialectic
    Sobriety of truth.

XVI

And if a long-held contest tended
    To ill-defined result,
It was by calm consent suspended
    As over-difficult :

XVII

And verse or music was suggested,
    Then solitude of night :
Whereby the senses are invested
    With spiritual sight.'

XVIII

So far, the city.   All around it,
    Olive, or vine, or corn ;
Those having pressed, or trod, or ground it,
    By these 'twas townward borne,

XIX

And placed in halls unbarred though splendid
   With none to overlook,
And whither each at leisure wended,
   And, what he wanted, took.

XX

And men saluted one the other,
   Or as they passed or stood,
" Let us still love and labour, brother;
   For life is sweet and good."

XXI

I saw no crippled forms nor meagre,
   None smitten by disease :
Only the old, nor loth nor eager,
   Dying by kind degrees.

XXII

And when, without or pain or trouble,
   They sank as sinks the sun,
" This is the sole Inevitable,"
   All said ; " His will be done !"

XXIII

And went, with music softly swelling,
   Where land o'erlooks the sea,
Over the corse piled herbs sweet-smelling,
   Consumed, and so set free.

XXIV

Past ocean wave and mountain daisy
  As curled the perfumed smoke,
The notes grew faint, the vision hazy :—
  Straining my sense, I woke.

*   *   *   *   *

XXV

SWIFT I arose.   Soft winds were stirring
  The curtains of the Morn,
Promise of day, by signs unerring,
  Lovely as e'er was born.

XXVI

But here the pleasant likeness ended
  Between the cities twain :
Level and straight these streets extended
  Over an easy plain.

XXVII

Withal, the people who thus early
  Began to troop and throng,
With curving back and visage surly
  Toiled painfully along.

XXVIII

Groups of them met at yet closed portals,
  And huddled round the gate,
Patient, as smit by the Immortals,
  And helots as by Fate.

XXIX

Full many a cross-crowned front and steeple
    Clave the cerulean air :
As grew the concourse of the people,
    They rang to rival prayer.

XXX

On their confronting walls were posted
    Placards in glaring type,
Whereof there was not one but boasted
    Truth full-grown, round, and ripe.

XXXI

And, with this self-congratulation,
    Each one the other banned,
With threats of durable damnation
    From the Eternal Hand.

XXXII

Surmounting these, were Forms forbidding
    Disputes about the Flood ;
Since, in such points divine unthridding,
    Shed had been human blood.

XXXIII

From arch and alley sodden wretches
    Crept out in half attire,
And groped for fetid husks and vetches
    · In heaps of tossed-out mire ;

XXXIV

Until disturbed by horses' trample,
   And faces fair and gay,
Which, sleek and warm, with ermines ample,
   And glittering diamond spray

XXXV

That lightly flecked the classic ripple
   Of their flower-scented hair,
For shivering child and leprous cripple
   Had not a look to spare.

XXXVI

In garments with the morn ill mated,
   Anon came youths along;
From side to side they oscillated,
   And trolled a shameful song.

XXXVII

Thereat my heart, this longwhile throbbing,
   With teardrops sought to ease
O'erwelling woe, and, wildly sobbing,
   I fell upon my knees.

XXXVIII

And made irreverent by the fluster
   Of sorrow's fierce extreme,
I cried, "O unjust Heaven! be juster,
   And realise my dream!"

XXXIX

Up streamed the sun, and straight were shining
    Steeple, and sill, and roof:
To my hot prayer and rash repining
    A visible reproof.

XL

Rebuked, I rose from genuflexion,
    And, ceasing to blaspheme,
Curtained mine eyes for introspection
    Of the departed dream,

XLI

Where men saluted one the other,
    In street, or field, or wood,
"Let us still love and labour, brother;
    For life is sweet and good."

XLII

And I resolved, by contrast smitten,
    To live and strive by Law;
And first to write, as here are written,
    The Visions Twain I saw.

A FRAGMENT

PART I

TO-DAY, and in this England! Wherefore not?
Shall the sepulchral yesterdays alone
Murmur of music, and our ears still lean
Toward sleeping stone for voices from the grave?
Back unto life, ye living! Nothing new
Under the sun? Say rather, nothing old.
Have the winds lost their freshness, or the Spring
One dimple of her beauty? Looks the moon,
Whom lovers will with tight-locked palms to-night
Gaze on in silence, by the silence hushed,
One hour less young than when o'er Trojan plains,
To Trojan eyes, she shepherded the stars?
Hero's true lamp is out; Leander's arms
No longer breast the barricading surge;
But beckoning lights still burn in lonely breasts,
And seas of separation moan unseen
'Twixt love and locked embraces, salter far
Than e'er embittered sweet Abydos' shore.

Let Delphi's fire be quenched ; fresh vapours rise
From smouldering hollows in the human heart,
Propounding riddles only verse can read.
Who understand not, ne'er had understood.

"Sheds all its golden gains upon the ground,
Leaving itself quite bare !"   Thus far, aloud,
Murmured Sir Alured, and then broke off,
Completing not his own mind's parallel.
For he was standing 'mid the smooth domain,
He newly called his own, his sire just dead,
And the year slowly dying, when his gaze
Paused at an ancient sycamore bereft
Of all its leaves, that lay upon the ground,
It black, they burnished, and had felt the shock
Of a too timely close comparison.
' Leaving itself quite bare !" again he sighed,
' Like the old arms of that too generous tree,
Whose latest, poorest, barest branch am I !"
Then strode he on, and gazed upon the earth,
As do we all when sadness with the soul
A silent parley holds, since that we know
Under the earth earth's sadness will be stilled.

Upon the crest, midway, of wooded ridge,
Stands brick-built Avoncourt, its feudal face
Set firmly toward the south, whose smile it takes
When smile is given ; but, when the skies are dim,
It wears on its indented front a look
Like battered armour.   Each fresh age hath striven

To keep it young and drape its rugged years
With gentler graces of the newer time.
Below the stone-girt terrace that recalls
Merlon and embrasure of sterner days,
Now softened down to peaceful purposes—
Peripatetic dialogue, or 'chance
The slow faint foot of some fair sentinel,
Who, since the voice she loves to list, not now
Murmurs unmeasured music in her ear,
Tells discreet night her secret and drinks in
The indefinite passion of the nightingale—
Stretch lake-like lawns, and islands of fair flowers.
Beyond, rolls wooded chase, where startled deer
With quick short jerks 'neath clean-lopped branches
        bound,
And in the bracken forest disappear,
Or upon open velvet spaces couched,
With antlers motionless and haunches sleek,
Consume the day in graceful idleness.
Its immemorial majesty of boughs
Shuts out the common world; but, should you stray
Past its exclusive precincts, you are lost,
Lost utterly in world of sprays and stems,
That ever and anon divide, and show
Long leafy cloisters where rapt silence prays
When no man's desecrating foot is there.

But though its woods, glades, pastures, still are fair,
Progress, that boastful spendthrift who eats up
The savings of the parsimonious Past,

Hath squandered all except its loveliness.
In time's fast growing legendary now,
When service was the other pole of sway,
On whose joint axis moved the duteous world,
The fief of Avoncourt was still alert
To furnish forth a knight, a horse, a shield,
And, on their feet, a modest retinue.
Then came the later and the laxer days,
When gentlehood, its armour doffing, stayed
Mildly at home, wielding a lazy rule,
And to poor mercenary starvelings left
The lists of honour.   With no foe to kill
Save time, who, killed, straight comes to life again,
Its desultory lords their lives despatched
'Twixt fox and flagon ; hunted, boozed, and slept,
More fatly fed and brawnier boors among
Big raw-boned boors, their brethren, who revered
With forelocks pulled a sceptre meaningless.
But when the New Age bustled into view,
And sleek evangelists with purse and scrip,
Converts to comfortable tenets, cried,
" Be rich and fear not !" and mankind received
The golden gospel with attentive ears,
And leaving father, mother, followed it,
Dominion's shadow slipped from Avoncourt.
It bore not, like the patriarch's spouse of old,
Within its womb a wonder late-conceived,
Such as in shires to north of Trent hath shed
On ostentatious plutocrats awhile
A counterfeited primacy which men

Will but to valorous wisdom long concede.
And so its race waxed insignificant;
Under the waves of opulence submerged,
And, since contending with the mounting tide,
More deeply drowned.

                    "A wealthy wife mends all.
Why not? It is the custom of the time.
I loiter out of fashion." As he spoke,
The staghound pacing gravely at his side
Gave a bound forward, and was suddenly lost.
He, freshly in his new-found thought entranced,
Walked on, and, heeding not the truant hound,
Let the path lead him, till the cloistered woods
Closed all around him, and on autumn leaves
He trod, with autumn leaves above his head.
But when the dream of mercenary bed
Waxed unto vivid nightmare, and he woke,
Catching his breath and asking was it true,
"Lufra!" he called, whistled, and waiting stood.
And lo! from out an aisle-like avenue
Came Lufra, slow, and on her grizzled head
A hand of white and tapering tenderness,
The index of a form he quickly scanned,
Fresh as a bud that just hath burst its sheath,
A fragrant blossom of May maidenhood.
"I have lost my way among these woods," she gasped
With a little laugh of shy perplexity,
And glancing round as though to run away,
Had she known where to run to. "Much I fear,

I trespass too." He, taken unawares
By the sharp contrast betwixt sordid dream
And fair reality, quickly exclaimed
Ere taking thought, " It were a churlish wood,
A churlish world, that deemed you trespasser !
Where would you go ?"

                        To maiden ear and heart
There nothing is in all the scale of sound
So sweet as unpremeditated praise ;
And he had lauded her unwittingly.
" I would go home ;" and therewithal she named
A cosy farm upon the southern verge
Of the land that called him lord, and told him how,
There 'mid the milk-sweet breath of homely kine,
Of cocks that crowed as though 'twere always dawn,
Of orchard-branches strung with coral fruit,
And porches cool with untrimmed honeysuckle,
She from the stale and stifling town had come,
To tend, as well as inexperience might,
Her mother's sister, only mother now.
" And may I be your guide ?"—" You must," she said,
" Unless you mean me to go rudderless
Through this big wood which is to me a sea,
Whereof I have not got the chart ; its paths,
Like to the waves, into each other fall,
Perplexing in their uniformity.
Do they not puzzle you ?"—" Me ? No," he said,
" I learned to thread them ere I learned that life
Hath any puzzles." Therewith walked they on,

Slim form by side of stalwart, mated well.
"Perhaps these woods are yours?" she said.   "They
    are.
"Is it not sad?"   For she had led him back
By that home question to the thought wherewith
His mind had started. "Sad?" she asked. "For whom?
For you, or for the woods?"—"Alas! for both."
Quick glancing up, she noticed that his garb
Symbolised sorrow.   "Sad, you mean, because
They fell to you but recently, and thus
Possession signifieth deeper loss."
"Ay, sad enough is that, but sadder still
When they who go but burden him that stays.
May we not doubt if stooping Atlas finds,
Too busy with his burden to look up,
The earth he shoulders, very beautiful?
The rivers roll above him, and the woods,
Leafier they are, the more they cumber him.
But look! a shore to your bewildering sea."

    And true, the pathway ended, stopped abrupt
By a gate that led into a field new-reaped,
Whereon were pheasants gleaning.   Here he leaned,
And she, because he was her guide, leaned too,
Gazing upon the scene, but he on her.
"How beautiful!" he murmured,—thinking of her;
While she, unconscious of his theme, and rapt
All in the scene, "How beautiful!" replied:
"How peaceful!"   And the music of her voice
Made music and peace in his unpeaceful heart.

Earth, our reputed Mother, so we lend
Our souls to her familiar influence
Wills not that any of her children be
To one another strangers ; and so close
Are we by instinct and dumb voice of blood,
That the harsh stepdame Custom ofttimes fails,
Even when girt with all its ceremony,
To keep us quite as alien as it would.
But when in lieu of jealous boundaries,
Of ambushed eyes, assassinating tongues,
And hearts expert in moral sophistry,
That from some lively premiss straight infer
Deadly conclusion, Nature's kindly troop,
The sky's ingenuous countenance, the frank,
The candid air, the unimputing woods,
The river flowing irresponsibly;
Make all our company, from them we draw
Contagious candour, and respond as free
As doth Æolian harp to hazard winds.

So, leaning there, with none to come between
The stirless autumn sunshine and their souls,
He, half to her, half to himself, resumed.
" Yes, they are mine, for that brief tenancy
Which we call life.   We are but tenants all,
Despite pretentious parchments, and my sires,
Whom death hath ousted from this holding, held
Under a kindlier landlord, that lost time,
Which we are told we ne'er shall find again,
When days and nights were easy, and men's deeds

And duties travelled along well-worn grooves,
Impalpable, yet certain as the track
On which revolve the seasons. Now, alas!
All grows uncertain and irregular.
None serves, none sways. We chaffer for our rights,
And haggle over service. Which pays best,
We ask, where all pays badly,—till we learn
That unpaid duty is best paid of all."

She listened; for believing youth that hears
Dark utterance, straight infers an oracle.
But he, aware he somewhat overmuch
Reflected autumn's abstract haziness,
Added, "Forgive me if I dreamed aloud,
And to a simple question gave you back
A round of riddles. Yes, the woods are mine.
Should I not rather say that I am theirs?"

Thereat, with little skill and no device,
But in that homely speech which moves us more
Than all the tropes of foreign rhetoric,
She said the very happiest lot on earth,
To her at least it seemed, was thus to be
Lord of the soil in England's lovely isle.
"Ay, ay," he said, sharp interrupting her,
"Its loveliness we kill not all at once,
Though many a rood, once fair and profitless,
To profitable foulness hath been warped,
And Nature every year pays heavier tax,
To wear her native livery. There you stand,

I   N

Rich in your youth, rich in your comeliness,
Their value undecreased by time or change ;
For comeliness and youth, ten æons hence,
Will be as young and comely and as prized
As they are now, while these poor woods will be
Burnt up to make some pandemonium puff
The smoke of Progress into Heaven's fixed face,
Or measured out in yards to serve as fringe
On thrifty Competition's narrow skirts.
Still they are mine, and I am theirs, and we
Must face the age together : cruel age,
Which makes men timid to be poor, withal
Still poorer, squandering life in dying rich."

"I thought the age we live in was," she said,
Still in response to scornful images
Tendering the words of meek simplicity,
"Reputed great.   I ever hear it praised,
Called wiser, better, more intelligent
Than all its sires.   But I am ignorant,
And only echo back the sounds I hear."
"We play with sounding words ; men ever did :
It is not children only love the drum ;"
Again with ready gibe he answered her.
"Progress :—but whither ?   Our contentions are
The wheels that carry Progress on its road.
But who is it that drives, and who that gains,
Because we still accelerate the pace ?
The axles of our poor revolving selves
Grow hot and hotter and still muddier ;

But never one inch nearer comes the goal.
How should it, when no pocket compass shows
Whether we go to, or away from, it?"

"God is the goal," she said, with reverent lips.
"Then being the goal, He must be stationary,
While we progress.   Do we progress towards Him?
Do railways, or with broad or narrow gauge,
Bring us one station nearer unto Heaven?
The electric leap, annihilating time,
As long as ever leaves Eternity;
And all its boasted currents, speed as far
As ere they can, bury themselves in earth,
And end their circuit where they started from."
Then, in a sadder tone, "O bootless round!
I do but see a motion meaningless,
With its monotonous mutability.
The years are linked to years, a lengthening chain;
But the hours wax not brighter, nor the days
Longer, nor yet the seasons fuller of hope."

"How sad you make the autumn afternoon!
And yet I cannot gladden it," she said.
"But others might, and, doing it, would plead
That Progress truer triumphs has to show
Than these, material, mechanical,
That leave us matter still.   Does thought not move?"
"It moves," he answered, "just as ocean moves,
Backward and forward; but its bulk remains
Long while unchanged, as do its boundaries.

Like architecture, thought would seem to have ta'en
All forms already that are possible.
Nought new is said, but only newly vamped :
And these pretentious novelties wherein   .
The upstart age struts proudly, are but gems
Carefully carven by an olden time,
Some cunning hand hath furbished up anew
And furnished with fresh setting."—"That sounds true,"
Gaining contentious courage, she replied :
" But metaphors well-chosen always do."
" Life is itself a metaphor," he said,
" Full of ambiguous meaning, striving still
To represent a something that is not.
We cannot get behind ourselves.   Thus, he
Who stands at the meridian of life,
Will count as much enlightenment behind
As in the future he anticipates.
The eye whose sun is setting deems mankind
Hath run its course of wisdom ; while the boy,
Since just out of his cradle, never doubts
That History backward is as dark as night,
And that the sunshine of the waking world
Is all to come.   All partial, and all, false.
If this be sad, then life hath little joy."

" Meanwhile we make no progress to *my* goal,"
She said with a smile.   So through the gate they passed,
Across the crackling stubble, onward thence
Over reaped aftermaths, bright emeralds set
In golden ring of autumn's circling woods ;

Over rude stile, with help of stronger hand,
First touch of palms whereby the spirit will oft
Send half-obscure electric messages,
Deciphered later.

Part II

" Loved me ?   Hath love a past then ?   What is that,
Once love, now love no longer? . . . Boastful fool !
Who is the victor now ?   These empty hands,
These empty halls, declare it, and I range
With farewell feet ancestral corridors,
With echo for my servitor. . . . Violet eyes,
And hair like sheaves of sunshine ; eyebrows broad,
Matching the tresses, arched, but outlined strong—
Not baby stencillings—'neath which, at times,
Broadened a gaze that seemed as looking out
Of all the Past at all Futurity.
Small dainty hands, as soft as captured bird,
So soft, we fear to crush it !—soft and white,
With feet to mate, fantastically fine,
True hint of her perfection, promised mine,
Now pawned another's for a sordid gain,
And ne'er to be redeemed !   O roof despised,
Withal so proud, that might have sheltered both,
And now must shelter neither, house thy ghosts,
My ancestors, and what I might have been,
Had woman's faith been fixed !   Now all things slip,
Past, present, future, down the gulf of time,

That whelms not me, who need must ride aloft
Upon its eddy, a still whirling leaf,
Too trivial to .drown !"

PART III

Deep thickets of green silence.   For it was
A summer noon, and summer was asleep,
And lent them welcome, but beheld them not.
Only themselves, and stillness, and the sweet
Shelter of interpenetrating boughs,
And bracken thick and footfalls unreturned
From the deep soft dry sheddings of the pine.

Deep down into her lucid eyes he gazed,
And clear he saw his image quivering there,
The shadow of his gazing and his thought.
For she was like a snow-fed lake that draws
Into its bosom only high-born streams ;
And he was like a cloudless night whose day
Has been the battlefield of clashing storms,
Raging, retreating, and returning still.
But now below the horizon were they gone,
And on her upward soul downward he shone,
With the serenity of a silent star.

AT SHELLEY'S HOUSE AT LERICI

I

MAIDEN, with English hair, and eyes
The colour of Italian skies,
    What seek you by this shore?
"I seek, sir, for the latest home
Where Shelley dwelt, and, o'er the foam
    Speeding, returned no more."

II

Come, then, with me : I seek it, too.
Are you his kith? For strangely you
    Resemble him in mien.
"No, save it be that all are kin
Who cherish the same thoughts within,
    And gaze on things unseen."

III

It should be easy, sure, to find.
Waves close in front, woods close behind,
    Green shutters, whitewashed walls ;

A little space of rocky ground,
Where climbs the wave, and, round and round
     The seagull curves and calls.

IV

Lo ! there it stands.   A quiet spot,
Untenanted, it seems forgot,
     Like shrine from which the God
Hath vanished, and but left behind
A something in the air, the wind,
     Recalling where he trod.

V

Upon this balcony how oft,
When waves were smooth and winds were soft,
     As now, he must have stood,
And dreamed of days when men should be
Bondless as this unfettered sea,
     And peaceful as that wood.

VI

What would he find if came he now ?
A phantom crown on kingly brow,
     Veiled sceptre, trembling throne ;
Pulpits where threat and curse have ceased,
And shrines whereat half-sceptic priest
     Worships, too oft, alone.

VII

With muffled psalm and whispered hymn,
At secret dawn or twilight dim,
  A pious remnant pray ;
For their maimed rites indulgence plead,
And, half uncertain of their creed,
  Explain their God away.

VIII

Gone the conventions Shelley cursed :
The first are last, the last are first ;
  The lame, the halt, the blind,
Now in the seat of power, along
With the far-seeing and the strong,
  Mould mandates for mankind.

IX

No longer doth man's will decide,
And woman's feebler impulse guide ;
  He yields to her his might :
Duty hath grown an old-world tale,
And chaste Obedience rends her veil,
  For epicene delight.

X

Where now do towering despots reign
Over lithe knee and servile brain,
  The scared, the base, the bought ?

Monarchs themselves now bend with awe
Before the kingliness of Law,
    The majesty of Thought.

XI

Yes, Kings have gone, or reign as slaves;
Religion mumbles round our graves,
    But shapes our lives no more :
Tradition, thrice-spurned Sibyl, burns
The leaves mob Sovereignty spurns,
    Contemptuous of her lore.

XII

Fair Maiden with the sea-blue eyes,
With whom, beneath these sea-blue skies,
    Shelley had loved to live,
Forgive me if his dream, unborn
Then, but now adult, moves my scorn :
    Would He too not forgive?

XIII

For where both Crown and Cowl defied
Sue for the ruth they once denied,
    What would he find instead?
A fiercer despot, fouler creed,
The Rule of Gold, the rites of Greed,
    And a bitterer cry for bread.

XIV

Wake, poet ! and retune your strings.
The earth now swarms with petty kings,
  Seated on self-made thrones,
And altar-tables richly spread,
Where Roguery consecrates the bread,
  And Opulence atones.

XV

Here Shelley prayed that War might cease
From earth, and Pentecostal Peace
  Descend with dovelike breath.
Look round this bay ! each treeless gorge,
Each scarred ravine, incessant forge
  The instruments of death.

XVI

From Salterbrand's unfreezing peaks
To sunny Manfredonia's creeks,
  Have alien satraps gone ;
But, guarding Italy the Free,
Her murderous mammoth-monsters, see,
  Come grimly wallowing on.

XVII

Yes, here He dwelt and dreamed : and there,
Gleams *Porto Venere* the fair,
  The mockery of a name.

Where fervent Venus once was Queen,
Hot Mars now ravishes the scene,
    And fans a fiercer flame.[1]

XVIII

Fair Maiden with the English brow,
Although from me, who shortly now
    Must tread life's downward slope,
Illusions one by one depart,
Still foster in your virgin heart
    The embryo of Hope.

XIX

The hills remain, the woods, the waves;
And they alone are dupes or slaves
    Who, spurning Nature's breast,
Too high would soar, too deep would sound,
And madden vainly round and round
    The orbit of unrest.

XX

Pity, too, lingers.   As I speak,
The teardrops tremble on your cheek,
    Too silent to deceive ;
And with assuaging hand you show
How tenderness still tempers woe,
    And none need singly grieve.

[1] The Bay of Spezia is now one vast arsenal, and one of the chief anchorages of the Italian Ironclad Squadron.

XXI

Yes! sweet it were, with you for guide,
To float across that dimpling tide,
 And, on its farther shore,
To prove if Venus still holds sway,
And, wandering with you round the bay,
 Tempt back one's youth once more.

XXII

But, child! it is not Shelley's world.
Fancy's light sails had best be furled,
 Before they surge and swell.
What helm can steer the heart? or who
Keep moored, inspired by such as You?
 Heaven prosper you! Farewell.

IN THE HEART OF THE FOREST

I

I HEARD the voice of my own true love
    Ripple the sunny weather.
Then away, as a dove that follows a dove,
    We flitted through woods together.

II

There was not a bush nor branch nor spray
    But with song was swaying and ringing.
" Let us ask of the birds what means their lay,
    And what is it prompts their singing."

III

We paused where the stichwort and speedwell grew
    'Mid a forest of grasses fairy :
From out of the covert the cushat flew,
    And the squirrel perched shy and wary.

IV

On an elm-tree top shrilled a misselthrush proud,
  Disdaining shelter or screening.
" Now what is it makes you pipe so loud,
  And what is your music's meaning?

V

" Your matins begin ere the dewdrop sinks
  To the heart of the moist musk-roses,
And your vespers last till the first star winks,
  And the vigilant woodreeve dozes."

VI

Then louder, still louder he shrilled : " I sing
  For the pleasure and pride of shrilling,
For the sheen and the sap and the showers of Spring
  That fill me to overfilling.

VII

" Yet a something deeper than Spring-time, though
  It is Spring-like, my throat keeps flooding :
Peep soft at my mate,—she is there below,—
  Where the bramble traiis are budding.

VIII

" She sits on the nest and she never stirs ;
  She is true to the trust I gave her ;
And what were my love if I cheered not hers
  As long as my throat can quaver?"

IX

So he quavered on, till asudden we heard
  A voice that called "Cuckoo!" and fleeted.
"Why all day is your name by yourself, vain bird,
  Repeated and still repeated?"

X

Then "Cuckoo! Cuck! Cuck! Cuck-oo!" he called,
  And he laughed and he chuckled cheerly;
"Your hearts they run dry and your heads grow bald,
  But I come back with April yearly.

XI

"I come in the month that is sweet, so sweet,
  Though its sweetness be frail and fickle,
In the season when shower and sunshine meet,
  And you reck not of Autumn's sickle.

XII

"I flout at the April loves of men
  And the kisses of shy fond maidens;
And then I call 'Cuckoo!' again, again,
  With a jeering and jocund cadence.

XIII

"When the hawthorn blows and the yaffel mates,
  I sing and am silent never;
Just as love of itself in the May-time prates,
  As though it will last for ever!

XIV

"And in June, ere I go, I double the note,
    As I flit from cover to cover:
Are not vows, at the last, repeated by rote
    By fading and fleeting lover?"

XV

A tear trickled down my true love's cheek
    At the words of the mocking rover;
She clung to my side, but she did not speak,
    And I kissed her over and over.

XVI

And while she leaned on my heart as though
    Her love in its depths was rooting,
There rose from the thicket behind us, slow,
    O such a silvery fluting!

XVII

When the long smooth note, as it seemed, must break,
    It fell in a swift sweet treble,
Like the sound that is made when a stream from a lake
    Gurgles o'er stone and pebble.

XVIII

And I cried, "O nightingale! tell me true,
    Is your music rapture or weeping?
And why do you sing the whole night through,
    When the rest of the world is sleeping?"

K

XIX

Then it fluted : " My notes are of love's pure strain,
    And could there be descant fitter ?
For why do you sever joy and pain,
    Since love is both sweet and bitter ?

XX

" My song now wails of the sighs, the tears,
    The long absence that makes love languish ;
Then thrills with its fluttering hopes and fears,
    Its rapture,—again its anguish.

XXI

"And why should my notes be hushed at night ?
    Why sing in the sunlight only ?
Love loves when 'tis dark, as when 'tis bright,
    Nor ceaseth because 'tis lonely."

XXII

My love looked up with a happy smile,
    (For a moment the woods were soundless) :
The smile of a heart that knows no guile,
    And whose trust is deep and boundless.

XXIII

And as I smiled that her smile betrayed
    The fulness of love's surrender,
Came a note from the heart of the forest shade,
    O·so soft, and smooth, and tender !

XXIV

'Twas but one note, and it seemed to brood
  On its own sufficing sweetness;
That cooed, and cooed, and again but cooed
  In a round, self-same completeness.

XXV

Then I said, "There is, ringdove, endless bliss
  In the sound that you keep renewing:
But have you no other note than this,
  And why are you always cooing?"

XXVI

The ringdove answered: "I too descant
  Of love as the woods keep closing;
Not of spring-time loves that exult and pant,
  But of harvest love reposing.

XXVII

"If I coo all day on the self-same bough,
  While the noisy popinjay ranges,
'Tis that love which is mellow keeps its vow,
  And callow love shifts and changes.

XXVIII

"When summer shall silence the merle's loud throat
  And the nightingale's sweet sad singing,
You still will hear my contented note,
  On the branch where I now am clinging.

XXIX

" For the rapture of fancy surely wanes,
  And anguish is lulled by reason ;
But the tender note of the heart remains
  Through all changes of leaf and season."

XXX

Then we plunged in the forest, my love and I,
  In the forest plunged deeper and deeper,
Till none could behold us save only the sky,
  Through a trellis of branch and creeper.

XXXI

And we paired and nested away from sight
  In a bower of woodbine pearly ;
And she broods on our love from morn to night,
  And I sing to her late and early.

XXXII

Nor till Death shall have stripped our lives as bare
  As the forest in wintry weather,
Will the world find the nest in the covert where
  We dwelt, loved, and sang together.

AT THE GATE OF THE CONVENT

I

BESIDE the Convent Gate I stood,
　Lingering to take farewell of those
To whom I owed the simple good
　Of three days' peace, three nights' repose.

II

My sumpter-mule did blink and blink;
　Was nothing more to munch or quaff;
Antonio, far too wise to think,
　Leaned vacantly upon his staff.

III

It was the childhood of the year:
　Bright was the morning, blithe the air;
And in the choir I plain could hear　　　˙
　The monks still chanting matin prayer.

IV

The throstle and the blackbird shrilled,
    Loudly as in an English copse,
Fountain-like note that, still refilled,
    Rises and falls, but never stops.

V

As lush as in an English chase,
    The hawthorn, guessed by its perfume,
With folds on folds of snowy lace
    Blindfolded all its leaves with bloom.

VI

Scarce seen, and only faintly heard,
    A torrent, 'mid far snow-peaks born,
Sang kindred with the gurgling bird,
    Flowed kindred with the foaming thorn.

VII

The chanting ceased, and soon instead
    Came shuffling sound of sandalled shoon;
Each to his cell and narrow bed
    Withdrew, to pray and muse till noon.

VIII

Only the Prior—for such their Rule—
    Into the morning sunshine came.
Antonio bared his locks; the mule
    Kept blinking, blinking, just the same.

IX

I thanked him with a faltering tongue ;
  I thanked him with a flowing heart.
" This for the poor."   His hand I wrung,
  And gave the signal to depart.

X

But still in his he held my hand,
  As though averse that I should go.
His brow was grave, his look was bland,
  His beard was white as Alpine snow.

XI

And in his eye a light there shone,
  A soft, subdued, but steadfast ray,
Like to those lamps that still burn on
  In shrines where no one comes to pray.

XII

And in his voice I seemed to hear
  The hymns that novice-sisters sing,
When only anguished Christ is near,
  And earth and life seem vanishing.

XIII

" Why do you leave us, dear my son ?
  Why from calm cloisters backward wend,
Where moil is much and peace is none,
  And journeying hath nor bourne nor end ?

XIV

" Read I your inmost soul aright,
   Heaven hath to you been strangely kind ;
Gave gentle cradle, boyhood bright,
   A fostered soul, a tutored mind.

XV

" Nor wealth did lure, nor penury cramp,
   Your ripening soul ; it lived and throve,
Nightly beside the lettered lamp,
   Daily in field, and glade, and grove.

XVI

" And when the dawn of manhood brought
   The hour to choose to be of those
Who serve for gold, or sway by thought,
   You doubted not, and rightly chose.

XVII

" Loving your Land, you face the strife ;
   Loved by the Muse, you shun the throng ;
And blend within your dual life
   The patriot's pen, the poet's song.

XVIII

" Hence now, in gaze mature and wise,
   Dwells scorn of praise, dwells scorn of blame ;
Calm consciousness of surer prize
   Than dying noise of living fame.

XIX

" Have you not loved, been loved, as few
　Love, or are loved, on loveless earth ?
How often have you felt its dew ?
　Say, have you ever known its dearth ?

XX

" I speak of love divorced from pelf,
　I speak of love unyoked and free,
Of love that deadens sense of self,
　Of love that loveth utterly.

XXI

" And this along your life hath flowed
　In full and never-failing stream,
Fresh from its source, unbought, unowed,
　Beyond your boyhood's fondest dream."

XXII

He paused.   The cuckoo called.   I thought
　Of English voices, English trees.
The far-off fancy instant brought
　The tears ; and he, misled by these,

XXIII

With hand upon my shoulder, said,
　" You own 'tis true.   The richest years
Bequeath the beggared heart, when fled,
　Only this legacy of tears.

XXIV

"Why is it that all raptures cloy?
    Though men extol, though women bless,
Why are we still chagrined with joy,
    Dissatisfied with happiness?

XXV

"Yes, the care-flouting cuckoo calls,
    And yet your smile betokens grief,
Like meditative light that falls
    Through branches fringed with autumn leaf.

XXVI

"Whence comes this shadow?   You are now
    In the full summer of the soul.
The answer darkens on your brow:
    'Winter the end, and death the goal.'

XXVII

"Yes, vain the fires of pride and lust
    Fierce in meridian pulses burn:
Remember, Man, that thou art dust,
    And unto dust thou shalt return.

XXVIII

"Rude are our walls, our beds are rough,
    But use is hardship's subtle friend.
He hath got all that hath enough;
    And rough feels softest, in the end.

XXIX

" While luxury hath this disease,
   It ever craves and pushes on.
Pleasures, repeated, cease to please,
   And rapture, once 'tis reaped, is gone.

XXX

" My flesh hath long since ceased to creep,
   Although the hairshirt pricketh oft.
A plank my couch ; withal, I sleep
   Soundly as he that lieth soft.

XXXI

" And meagre though may be the meal
   That decks the simple board you see,
At least, my son, we never feel
   The hunger of satiety.

XXXII

" You have perhaps discreetly drunk :
   O, then, discreetly, drink no more !
Which is the happier, worldling, monk,
   When youth is past, and manhood o'er ?

XXXIII

" Of life beyond I speak not yet.
   'Tis solitude alone can e'er,
By hushing controversy, let
   Man catch earth's undertone of prayer.

XXXIV

"Your soul which Heaven at last must reap,
   From too much noise hath barren grown ;
Long fallow silence must it keep,
   Ere faith revive, and grace be sown.

XXXV

"Let guide and mule alone return.
   For you I will prepare a cell,
In whose calm silence you will learn,
   Living or dying, All is well !"

XXXVI

Again the cuckoo called ; again
   The merle and mavis shook their throats ;
The torrent rambled down the glen,
   The ringdove cooed in sylvan cotes.

XXXVII

The hawthorn moved not, but still kept
   As fixedly white as far cascade ;
The russet squirrel frisked and leapt
   From breadth of sheen to breadth of shade.

XXXVIII

I did not know the words had ceased,
   I thought that he was speaking still,
Nor had distinguished sacred priest
   . From pagan thorn, from pagan rill.

XXXIX

Not that I had not harked and heard;
  But all he bade me shun or do,
Seemed just as sweet as warbling bird,
  But not more grave and not more true.

XL

So deep yet indistinct my bliss,
  That when his counsels ceased to sound,
That one sweet note I did not miss
  From other sweet notes all around.

XLI

But he, misreading my delight,
  Again with urging accents spoke.
Then I, like one that's touched at night,
  From the deep swoon of sweetness woke.

XLII

And just as one that, waking, can
  Recall the thing he dreamed, but knows
'Twas of the phantom world that man
  Visits in languors of repose;

XLIII

So, though I straight repictured plain
  All he had said, it seemed to me,
Recalled from slumber, to retain
  No kinship with reality.

XLIV

"Father, forgive !" I said ; "and look !
Who taught its carolling to the merle ?
Who wed the music to the brook ?
Who decked the thorn with flakes of pearl ?

XLV

"'Twas He, you answer, that did make
Earth, sea, and sky : He maketh all ;
The gleeful notes that flood the brake,
The sad notes wailed in Convent stall.

XLVI

"And my poor voice He also made ;
And like the brook, and like the bird,
And like your brethren mute and staid,
I too can but fulfil His word.

XLVII

"Were I about my loins to tie
A girdle, and to hold in scorn
Beauty and Love, what then were I
But songless stream, but flowerless thorn ?

XLVIII

"Why do our senses love to list
When distant cataracts murmur thus ?
Why stealeth o'er your eyes a mist
When belfries toll the Angelus ?

XLIX

" It is that every tender sound
  Art can evoke, or Nature yield,
Betokens something more profound,
  Hinted, but never quite revealed.

L

"And though it be the self-same Hand
  That doth the complex concert strike,
The notes, to those that understand,
  Are individual, and unlike.

LI

" Allow my nature.   All things are,
  If true to instinct, well and wise.
The dewdrop hinders not the star ;
  The waves do not rebuke the skies.

LII

" So leave me free, good Father dear,
  While you on humbler, holier chord
Chant your secluded Vespers here,
  To fling my matin notes abroad.

LIII

" While you with sacred sandals wend
  To trim the lamp, to deck the shrine,
Let me my country's altar tend,
  Nor deem such worship less divine.

LIV

" Mine earthly, yours celestial love :
      Each hath its harvest ; both are sweet.
You wait to reap your Heaven, above ;
      I reap the Heaven about my feet.

LV

" And what if I—forgive your guest
      Who feels, so frankly speaks, his qualm—
Though calm amid the world's unrest,
      Should restless be amid your calm ?

LVI

" But though we two be severed quite,
      Your holy words will sound between
Our lives, like stream one hears at night,
      Louder, because it is not seen.

LVII

" Father, farewell !   Be not distressed ;
      And take my vow, ere I depart,
To found a Convent in my breast,
      And keep a cloister in my heart."

LVIII

The mule from off his ribs a fly
      Flicked, and then zigzagged down the road.
Antonio lit his pipe, and I
      Behind them somewhat sadly strode.

LIX

Just ere the Convent dipped from view,
    Backward I glanced : he was not there.
Within the chapel, well I knew,
    His lips were now composed in prayer.

LX

But I have kept my vow.   And when
    The cuckoo chuckleth o'er his theft,
When throstles sing, again, again,
    And runnels gambol down the cleft,

LXI

With these I roam, I sing with those,
    And should the world with smiles or jeers
Provoke or lure, my lids I close,
    And draw a cowl about my ears.

ι

BROTHER BENEDICT

I

BROTHER BENEDICT rose and left his cell
With the last slow swing of the evening bell.
In his hand he carried his only book,
And he followed the path to the Abbey brook,
And, crossing the stepping-stones, paused midway,
For the journeying water seemed to say,
                                    Benedicite.

II

But when he stood on the other bank,
The flags rose tall, and the grass grew rank,
And the sorrel red and the white meadow-sweet
Shook their dust on his sandalled feet,
And, lifting their heads where his girdle hung,
Would surely have said had they found a tongue,
                                    Benedicite.

III

Onward and upward he clomb and wound,
Bruising the thyme on the nibbled ground

Here and there, in the untrimmed brake,
The dog-rose bloomed for its own sweet sake ;
The woodbine clambered up out of reach,
But the scent of them all breathed as plain as speech,
Benedicite.

IV

Shortly he came to a leafy nook,
Where wind never entered nor branch ever shook.
Itself was the only thing in sight,
And the rest of the world was shut out quite.
'Twas as self-contained as the holy place
Where the children quire with upturned face,
Benedicite.

V

A dell so curtained with trunks and boughs,
That in hours when the ringdove coos to his spouse,
The sun to its heart scarce a way could win.
But the trees now had drawn all their shadows in ;
There was nothing but scent in the dewy air,
And the silence seemed saying in mental prayer,
Benedicite.

VI

'Gainst the trunk of a beech, round, smooth, and gray,
Brother Benedict leaned, with intent to pray,
And opened his book : with vellum bound ;
Within, red letters on faded ground ;
Pater, and Ave, and saving Creed :—
But look where you would, you seemed to read,
Benedicite.

VII

He scarce had a verse of his office said,
Ere a bird in the branches overhead
Began to warble so sweet a strain,
That, strive as he would, still he strove in vain
To close his ears; so he closed his book,
While the unseen throat to the air outshook
                                        Benedicite.

VIII

'Twas a song that rippled, and revelled, and ran
Ever back to the note whence it began;
Rising, and falling, and never did stay,
Like a fountain that feeds on itself all day,
Wanting no answer, answering none,
But beginning again as each verse was done,
                                        Benedicite.

IX

It brought an ecstasy into his face,
It weaned his senses from time and space,
It carried him off to worlds unseen,
And showed him what is not and ne'er has been,
Transporting his soul to those realms of calm,
More blessèd and blessing than even the psalm,
                                        Benedicite.

X

Then, carolling still, it drew him thence
Slowly back to the spheres of sense,
But held him awhile where self expires,

And vague recollections and vague desires
Banish the burden of things that are,
And angels seem canticling, faint and far,
                                        Benedicite.

XI

Then across him there flitted the days that are dead,
And those that will follow when these are fled;
Generations of sorrow, wave after wave,
With their samesome journey from womb to grave;
Men's love of the fleshly sweets that sting,
And the comfort that comes when we kneel and sing,
                                        Benedicite.

XII

He suddenly started and gazed around,
For silence can waken as well as sound,
And the bird had ceased singing. The dewy air
Still was immersed in mental prayer.
Time seemed to have stopped. So he quickened pace,
But forgot not to say ere he left the lone place,
                                        Benedicite.

XIII

Downward he wended, and under his feet,   .
As on mounting, the bruised thyme answered sweet;
As before, in the brake the dog-rose bloomed,
And the woodbine with fragrance the hedge perfumed;
And the white meadow-sweet and the sorrel red,
Had they found a tongue, would still surely have said,
                                        Benedicite.

XIV

But where were the flags and the tall rank grass,
And the stepping-stones smooth for his feet to pass?
Were they swept away?   Did he wake or dream?
A bridge that he knew not spanned the stream;
Though under its archway he still could hear
The journeying water purling clear,
>   Benedicite.

XV

Where had he wandered?   This never could
Be the spot where the Abbey orchard stood?
Where the filberts once mellowed, lay tumbled blocks,
And cherry stumps peered through tares and docks;
A rough plot stretched where in times gone by
The plump apples dropped to the joyous cry,
>   Benedicite.

XVI

The gateway had vanished, the portal flown,
The walls of the Abbey were ivy-grown;
The arches were shattered, the roof was gone,
The mullions were mouldering one by one;
Wrecked was the oriel's tracery light
That the sun streamed through when they met to recite
>   Benedicite.

XVII

Chancel and choir and nave and aisle
Were but one ruinous vacant pile.

So utter the havoc, you could not tell .
Which was corridor, cloister, cell.
Cow-grass, and foxglove, and waving weed,
Covered the scrolls where you used to read,

Benedicite.

XVIII

High up where of old the belfry towered,
An elder had rooted and whitely flowered :
Surviving ruin and rain and wind,
Below it a lichened gurgoyle grinned.
Though birds were chirping and flitting about,
They paused not to treble the anthem devout,

Benedicite.

XIX

Then he went where the Abbot was wont to lay
His children to rest till the Judgment Day,
And at length in the grass the name he found
Of a friar he fancied alive and sound.
The slab was hoary, the carving blurred,
And he rather guessed than could read the word,

Benedicite.

XX

He sate him down on a fretted stone,
Where rains had beaten and winds had blown,
And opened his office-book, and read
The prayers that we read for our loved ones dead,
While nightfall crept on the twilight air,
And darkened the page of the final prayer, ˙

Benedicite.

XXI

But to murkiest gloom when the gloaming did wane,
In the air there still floated a shadowy strain.
'Twas distilled with the dew, it was showered from the
　　star,
It was murmuring near, it was tingling afar ;
In silence it sounded, in darkness it shone,
And in sleep that is deepest it wakeful dreamed on,
　　　　　　　　　　　　Benedicite.

XXII

Do you ask what had witched Brother Benedict's ears ?
The bird had been singing a thousand years :
Sweetly confounding in its sweet lay
To-day, to-morrow, and yesterday.
Time ?　What is Time but a fiction vain,
To him that o'erhears the Eternal strain,
　　　　　　　　　　　　Benedicite ?

IN THE MONTH WHEN SINGS
THE CUCKOO

I

Hark! Spring is coming. Her herald sings,
                              Cuckoo !
The air resounds and the woodland rings,
                              Cuckoo ! Cuckoo !
Leave the milking pail and the mantling cream,
And down by the meadow, and up by the stream,
Where movement is music and life a dream,
          In the month when sings the cuckoo.

II

Away with old Winter's frowns and fears,
                              Cuckoo ! Cuckoo !
Now May with a smile dries April's tears.
                              Cuckoo !
When the bees are humming in bloom and bud,
And the kine sit chewing the moist green cud,
Shall the snow not melt in a maiden's blood,
          In the month when sings the cuckoo ?

III

The popinjay mates and the lapwing woos;
                    Cuckoo!
In the lane is a footstep.   I wonder whose?
                    Cuckoo! Cuckoo!
How sweet are low whispers! and sweet, so sweet,
When the warm hands touch and the shy lips meet,
And sorrel and woodruff are round our feet,
          In the month when sings the cuckoo.

IV

Your face is as fragrant as moist musk-rose;
                    Cuckoo! Cuckoo!
All the year in your cheek the windflower blows;
                    Cuckoo! Cuckoo!
You flit as blithely as bird on wing;
And when you answer, and when they sing,
I know not if they, or You, be Spring,
          In the month when pairs the cuckoo.

V

Will you love me still when the blossom droops?
                    Cuckoo!
When the cracked husk falls and the fieldfare troops?
                    Cuckoo!
Let sere leaf or snowdrift shade your brow,
By the soul of the Spring, sweet-heart, I vow,
I will love you then as I love you now,
          In the month when sings the cuckoo.

VI

Smooth, smooth is the sward where the loosestrife grows,
Cuckoo ! Cuckoo !

As we lie and hear in a dreamy doze,
Cuckoo ! Cuckoo ! Cuckoo !

And smooth is the curve of a maiden's cheek,
When she loves to listen but fears to speak,
And we yearn but we know not what we seek,
In the month when sings the cuckoo.

VII

But in warm mid summer we hear no more,
Cuckoo !

And August brings not, with all its store,
Cuckoo !

When Autumn shivers on Winter's brink,
And the wet wind wails through crevice and chink,
We gaze at the logs, and sadly think
Of the month when called the cuckoo.

VIII

But the cuckoo comes back and shouts once more,
Cuckoo !

And the world is as young as it was before;
Cuckoo ! Cuckoo !

It grows not older for mortal tears,
For the falsehood of men or for women's fears;
'Tis as young as it was in the bygone years,
When first was heard the cuckoo.

IX

I will love you then as I love you now.
                              Cuckoo !
What cares the Spring for a broken vow ?
                         Cuckoo ! Cuckoo !
The broods of last year are pairing, this ;
And there never will lack, while love is bliss,
Fresh ears to cozen, fresh lips to kiss,
              In the month when sings the cuckoo.

X

O cruel bird ! will you never have done ?
        .   Cuckoo ! Cuckoo ! Cuckoo !
You sing for the cloud, as you sang for the sun ;
                         Cuckoo ! Cuckoo !
You mock me now as you mocked me then,
When I knew not yet that the loves of men
Are as brief as the glamour of glade and glen,
              And the glee of the fleeting cuckoo.

XI

O, to lie once more in the long fresh grass,
                              Cuckoo !
And dream of the sounds and scents that pass ;
                         Cuckoo ! Cuckoo !
To savour the woodbine, surmise the dove,
With no roof save the far-off sky above,
And a curtain of kisses round couch of love,
              While distantly called the cuckoo.

XII

But if now I slept, I should sleep to wake
To the sleepless pang and the dreamless ache,
To the wild babe blossom within my heart,
To the darkening terror and swelling smart,
To the searching look and the words apart,
   And the hint of the tell-tale cuckoo.

XIII

The meadow grows thick, and the stream runs deep,
      Cuckoo!
Where the aspens quake and the willows weep;
      Cuckoo! Cuckoo!
The dew of the night and the morning heat
Will close up the track of my farewell feet :—
So good-bye to the life that once was sweet,
   When so sweetly called the cuckoo.

XIV

The kine are unmilked, and the cream unchurned,
      Cuckoo!
The pillow unpressed, and the quilt unturned,
      Cuckoo! Cuckoo!
'Twas easy to gibe at a beldame's fear
For the quick brief blush and the sidelong tear;
But if maids will gad in the youth of the year,
   They should heed what says the cuckoo.

XV

There are marks in the meadow laid up for hay,
                                    Cuckoo !
And the tread of a foot where no foot should stray :
                                    Cuckoo ! Cuckoo !
The banks of the pool are broken down,
Where the water is quiet and deep and brown ;—
The very spot, if one longed to drown,
        And no more to hear the cuckoo.

XVI

'Tis a full taut net and a heavy haul.
                                    Cuckoo ! Cuckoo !
Look ! her auburn hair and her trim new shawl !
                                    Cuckoo ! Cuckoo !
Draw a bit this way where 'tis not so steep ;
There, cover her face !   She but seems asleep ;
While the swallows skim and the graylings leap,
        And joyously sings the cuckoo.

LOVE'S WIDOWHOOD

I

Now I who oft have carolled of the Spring,
Must chant of Autumn and the dirgeful days ;
Of windless dawns enveiled in dewy haze,
Of cloistered evenings when no sweet birds sing,
But every note of joy hath trooped and taken wing.

II

But when I saw Her first, you scarce could say
If it were Summer still, or Autumn yet.
Rather it seemed as if the twain had met,
And, Summer being loth to go away,
Autumn retained its hand, and begged of it to stay.

III

The second bloom had come upon the rose,
Not, as in June, exultingly content
With its own loveliness, but meekly bent,
Pondering how beauty saddens to the close,
And fair decay consumes each hectic flower that blows.

IV

The traveller's-joy still journeyed in the hedge,
Nor yet to palsied gossamer had shrunk :
Green still the bracken round the beech-tree's trunk';
But loosestrife seeded by the river ledge,
And now and then a sigh came rippling through the
    sedge.

V

The white-cupped bindweed garlanded the lane,
Trying to make-believe the year was young.
Withal, hard-by, where it too clomb and clung,
The berried bryony began to wane,
And the wayfaring-tree showed many a russet stain.

VI

There was a pensive patience in the air,
As sweet as sad, when sadness doth but flow
From generous grief, and not for selfish woe :
Such as can make the wrinkled forehead fair,
And sheds a halo round love's slowly-silvering hair.

VII

And such She seemed. The summer in her mien
Had something too of autumn's mellower tone ;
A something that was more surmised than shown,
As when, though distant woodlands still are green,
Embrowning shadows seem half stealing in between.

VIII

Then, in that season, She alone with me,
As when the world was virginal and young,
Went wandering slowly, pathlessly, among
Fair scenes it made you happy but to see,
And wish that as they were they ever still might be.

IX

Sometimes we lingered at a rustic seat,
To listen to the soothing music made
By uninstructed breezes as they played
Upon the mellow pipes of waving wheat,
Nor spake, but only smiled, the music was so sweet.

X

But when anew we thither came, we found
The swarthy reapers, like their sickles, bent
Among the stalks whose summer now was spent.
Soon the light swathes in heavy sheaves were bound,
And tawny tents of peace stood dotted o'er the ground.

XI

And when the hinds departed with their hooks,
And no rude voices hurt the silence there,
We to the spot together would repair,
And, carrying thither bread, and fruit, and books,
Make for ourselves a seat against the sheltering stooks.

M   N

XII

There would she read to me some simple tale
Of love and sorrow, which, being simply told,
And softly read, both saddened and consoled.
    Whereat her voice would falter, cheek would pale,
And in her tender eyes the pity-drops prevail.

XIII

Oft would she bid me, when the light grew less,
Read or recite what poets weave in rhyme :
For verse, she said, doth not grow old with time,
    And sheds a solemn glamour round distress,
Until grief almost seems akin to happiness.

XIV

When came the heavy slowly-creaking wain,
And, one by one the stooks being wheeled away,
There now seemed nothing there but yesterday,
    Onward we wandered over stubbled plain
Till rows of ripened hop replaced the garnered grain.

XV

There for awhile it pleasant was to lean
Against some time-warped gate, and watch the folk,
Whose gay patched garb their lowliness bespoke,
    Stripping the fruitage from the alleys green,
While children romped or slept amid the busy scene.

XVI

Then did the sickle of the harvest moon
Its curve complete, and round itself with light,
Rising at sunset to retard the night.
Thrice thus it came, nor later nor more soon,
And thrice I hailed its disc, and begged of it a boon.

XVII

"O mellow moon, moon of plump stacks, and boughs
Blooming with fruit more juicy than the Spring,
Thee will I worship, thee henceforth will sing,
If thou wilt only listen to my vows,
And grant my sobering heart a home and harvest spouse."

XVIII

For, in those wanderings ne'er to be forgot,
My heart went out to her and came not back:
So that a something now I seemed to lack
Whene'er I wandered where she wandered not,
That wizarded away enchantment from the spot.

XIX

But I the ferment in my day-dream chid,
And brooded on it with a silent breast.
So quietly love sat upon its nest,
That, though she was so near to it, she did
Not see nor yet surmise where it lay hushed and hid.

XX

The cottage where she dwelt was long and low,
With sloping red-tiled roof and gabled front,
And timbered eaves that broke the weather's brunt
Ask you its age and date?　None cared to know,
Save 'twas that goodly time which men call Long-ago.

XXI

And each new generation, as it chose,
Added a dormer there, a gable here,
So had it grown more human year by year.
It had a look of ripeness and repose,
And up its kindly walls there clambered many a rose.

XXII

And sooth a constant smile it well might wear,
For on a garden ever did it gaze,
That still decoyed the sunshine's shifting rays,
And bloomed with flowers which brightened so the
　　air,
That folks who passed would halt and wish their home
　　was there.

XXIII

Old-fashioned balsams, snapdragons red and white,
In which the sedulous bees all day were throng,
Hastening from each, too busy to stay long;
Wise evening-primroses, that shun strong light,
But kindle with the stars and commerce with the night

XXIV

Moon-daisies tall, and tufts of crimson phlox,
And dainty white anemones that bear
An eastern name, and eastern beauty wear;
Lithe haughty lilies, homely-smelling stocks,
And sunflowers green and gold, and gorgeous holly-
    hocks.

XXV

In truth there is no flower nor leaf that breathes,
But found a hospitable shelter there,   .
Being fondly fostered, so that it was fair.
Near proud gladioli with formal sheaths,
Loose woodbine clomb and fell in long unfettered
    wreaths.

XXVI

Full many a flower there was you had not found,
Save for the scent its modesty exhaled.
When noonday heat or gloaming dews prevailed,
A fragrant freshness floated from the ground,
And smell of mignonette was everywhere around.

XXVII

Behind it was a pleasance free from weeds,
Where every household herb and tuber grew :
Kale of all kinds, bediamonded with dew,
Each quick green crop that quick green crop
    succeeds,
And all nutritious plants that prosper for man's needs.

XXVIII

But here no less did flowers abound, with fruits
That in September are themselves like flowers:
Rows of sweet-pea and honeysuckle bowers;
Red rustic apples, pears in russet suits,
And china-asters prim, and medlar's trailing shoots.

XXIX

There too grew southernwood, for courtship's aid,
And faithful lavender, one happy May
Brought from the garden of Anne Hathaway.
For human wants can thus be comely made,
And use with beauty dwell, unshamed and unafraid.

XXX

Beyond it was an orchard thick with trees,
·Whose branches now were bowed down to the ground
By clustering pippins, juicy, plump and sound,
Where it was sweet to saunter at one's ease,
Screened from too sultry rays, or sheltered from the
          breeze.

XXXI

Beside it ran a long straight alley green,
Paven with turf and vaulted in with leaves;
Whither, on idle mornings, restful eves,
You might repair, and, pacing all unseen,
Muse on twin life and death, and ponder what they
     . mean.

XXXII

Now that with bulging sacks the farmer clomb
His oast-house steps, and corn-stacks clustered round,
And shrivelled bine lay twisted on the ground,
We less than hitherto were lured to roam,
But in that pleasance stayed, and lingered round her
    home:

XXXIII

Gathering the last ripe peaches on the wall,
Splitting the pears to see if they were fit
Yet to be stored; or haply we would sit,
Watch the slow team returning to the stall,
Feel the soft shadows float, and hear the acorns fall.

XXXIV

It happed, one day, as we sat silent there,
Since silence seemed still sweeter than discourse,
My welling heart upbubbled from its source,
And I besought if she with me would share
The sweet sad load of life we all of us must bear.

XXXV

A something slumbering deep in her, slowly woke,
Then tranquilly she laid her hand on mine,
As though to hush, yet heal, me by that sign.
And, as her quiet voice the quiet broke,
It seemed as though it was grave Autumn's self that
    spoke.

XXXVI

"Of gifts, Love is the fairest, rarest, best,
And what you proudly give I cannot choose
But humbly take : 'twere vileness to refuse.
Giving, you grow no poorer, I more blest,
And that which I accept, by you is still possessed.

XXXVII

"For love, true love, doth give not that it may
In turn receive, only that it may give,
And on its careless lavishness doth live ;
Squandering itself, grows richer day by day,
Wealthiest in wealth when it hath given it all away.

XXXVIII

"And my, my love I carried not to mart,
In the fresh bloom and April of my days.
Rather the bloom was April's less than May's.
For though the Spring still carolled in my heart,
Summer's more steadfast thoughts had there begun to
       start.

XXXIX

"What then I gave I ne'er have taken back,
And so have not impoverishëd my life,
Nor set my present with my past at strife.
However long or lonely be the track,
Love strays not from its road nor faints beneath its pack.

XL

"Dead? Is he dead? how could he die, or be
Other than living unto love whose breath
Defends whate'er it breathes upon from death?
Therefore so long as *I* live, so must he,
Warmed by my warmth and fed by it perpetually.

XLI

"Change? Did he change? How could he change,
        or lose
The glory love once rayed around his hair?
The years have gone, the halo still is there.
There is no art like Love's, for it imbues
Its form with lasting light and never-fading hues.

XLII

"Why doth he come not? Wherefore should he come,
Who never from my side can go away?
His is the first face seen when dawns the day,
His the voice heard when birds sing or bees hum,
And his the presence felt when night is dark and dumb.

XLIII

"As I have loved, so surely you will love,
Drawn hither oft, and never here denied;
Constant as, when all springtime hopes have died,
The low unanswered coo of woodland dove,
Though no thrush pipes below and no lark trills above.

XLIV

"And should you come, and should you care to hear,
I in some timely hour will tell you more
Of my Love's Widowhood, never told before.
The tale will fall upon a kindred ear,
And with its sadness suit the autumn of the year."

XLV

So nowise less I thitherward was drawn,
Crossing at will her threshold late and soon,
But oftenest in the slanting afternoon,
When lay the long grave shadows on the lawn,
Lingering till gleamed the star that hails both dark and
        dawn.

XLVI

But since there something was to say, unsaid,
And time for saying it had come not yet,
We mostly now, as when we first had met,
Would saunter forth with desultory tread,
And roam where winding lane or alleyed coppice led.

XLVII

Sometimes we brought our simple childhood back
By gathering blackberries, now purpling fast;
Playing at which of us should show at last
The largest store, and ripest, and most black;
Then, serious grown once more, we took our homeward
        track.

XLVIII

Anon it pleased our fancy to explore
The hedgerow banks for some belated flower
That comes in flocks in April's magic hour ;
Primrose, or vetch, or violet, that wore
The smile of bygone days, or omened those before.

XLIX

These having found, and with them one wild rose
That wafted back the scent of summer days,
And shamed the bramble with its lovelier gaze,
I made a posy fresh and young as those
That children carry home when ladysmocks unclose.

L

Protesting love and beauty grow not old,
And in November twilight throstles sing.
" 'Tis only Autumn dreaming of the Spring,
That soon must wake to Winter's clammy cold,"
She answered me, as one whom sadness best consoled.

LI

" Gather me seasonable blooms," she said,
" For autumn flowers befit an autumn heart.
They do not mean to linger, but depart.
See ! the bur-marigold now droops its head,
And scabious withered stoops, slow tottering towards its
    bed.

LII

"Gather me these : I love each waning bloom ;
The berried bryony's discoloured bine,
The scarlet hips of scentless eglantine ;
The intrepid bramble, conscious of its doom,
That blends with fruit late flowers, to decorate its tomb.

LIII

" These to the tender heart are not less dear,
Because they mind of life's maturing debt.
Look where the honeysuckle lingers yet,
Curving an arm about the agëd year,
That gazes back its thanks through an autumnal tear."

LIV

When, on the morrow of that day, I went
Again to listen to her voice, she drew
Slowly my footsteps where no rude wind blew,
And, in the shelter of a leafy tent,
Her promised tale began, nor·paused till it was spent.

LV

" It was the season when the bluebell takes
The place the waning primrose vacant leaves,
When whistling starlings build behind the eaves,
When in the drowsy hive the bee awakes,
When daisies fleck the meads and blackbirds throng the
·brakes :

LVI

" When wails the nightingale lest we be made,
Hearing the cuckoo's jocund note, too glad,
But even sadness is not wholly sad ;
When Hope shoots fresh to cover hopes decayed,
And young Love walks abroad, alone and unafraid :

LVII

" When dykes are silvery runnels that skip and sing
To flowers that lean and listen the whole day long,
And life is nourished but on scent and song.
Then was it that He came, and seemed to fling
A superadded spell and splendour round the Spring.

LVIII

" I loved him as one loves the music brought
By sylvan streams where other sound is none ;
I loved him as one loves the lavish sun,
That scatters itself unbidden and unbought,
Or as one loves some great unmercenary thought.

LIX

" I was too buoyed on bliss that was, to deem
Of bane that might be ; for the present gave
More than the past had ever dared to crave.
Onward I floated in a trustful dream,
Like one that sails adown some music-murmuring stream.

LX

" But it was in no noonday dream I saw
A woman stand before me, calm and cold,
Like to those statues that men carved of old,
Majestic, abstract, without fleck or flaw,
That turn away from love, and dominate by awe.

LXI

" Her marble womb conceived him, and she claimed
His breath, and pulse, and will, as still her own ;
A being for her purpose got and grown,
As she wished wishing, aiming as she aimed,
And whom none else must touch, that wished to live
    unblamed.

LXII

" And when I pleaded vow, and faith, and trust,
She girded I had. filched his troth by stealth,
And that I prized him, not for worth, but wealth :
With every cruel stroke and cynic thrust
Maiming Love's heavenward wing, to trail it in the dust.

LXIII

" Thereat I did not lower but raised my head,
And high my scorn towered up above her scorn.
' O woman surely not of woman born,
A woman shall redress this wrong,' I said :
' Keep what you claim as yours ; your son I will not wed.'

LXIV

" And I have kept my pledge alike to both ;
Gave what he asked, and what she banned withheld,
Love unrecanted, but my pride unquelled.
I scorned all bond save love's unwritten troth,
Trusting the living link engrafted on its growth.

LXV

" Nay, do not pity, or with pity blend
The frown that like a shadow still follows wrong.
Brief was the rapture, the repentance long.
When pride that soars hath towered but to descend,
Then humble duty proves life's only lasting friend.

LXVI

" But, while you blame, yet blame not overmuch,
Since 'twas not baseness which begot that fault.
Where prudence hesitates, I did not halt :
What marriage deems its own, I scorned to clutch,
And virgin kept my heart from every venal touch.

LXVII

" At least I loved : not loved as women do,
Who weigh their hearts in nicely-balanced scale,
Careful lest gift should over gain prevail ; ·
But no more dreaming those should bribe who woo,
Than ringdove in the copse that answers coo with coo.

LXVIII

"Nor did I mete out love as though it be
A thing to bear division, and to dole
In labelled fragments, body, heart, and soul;
Withholding any of that triune three,
Yielding this one in full, and that but grudgingly.

LXIX

"Soul, heart, and body, we thus singly name,
Are not, in love, divisible and distinct,
But each with each inseparably linked.
One is not honour, and the other shame,
But burn as closely fused as fuel, heat, and flame.

LXX

"They do not love who give the body and keep
The heart ungiven; nor they who yield the soul,
And guard the body. Love doth give the whole;
Its range being high as heaven, as ocean deep,
Wide as the realms of air or planet's curving sweep.

LXXI

" And thus it was I loved; reserving not
One element of all Self has to give,
And in another's happiness did live;
Like to a flower that, rooted to one spot,
Yields sun and dew the scent that dew and sun begot.

LXXII

"Mourn not that love is blind. If love could see,
Love then would scarce be love. Its bandaged eyes
Gaze inward, and behold in clearest guise
The object of its thought, which, since they be
Seen thus, appear more real than blurred reality.

LXXIII

"And Love surrenders not its dream even when
Life draws the curtain of its sleep, and cries,
'Awake! behold the day with dreamless eyes!'
But wanders mournful 'mid the ways of men,
Missing the thing it seeks, nor hopes to find again.

LXXIV

"Thus can I never make a pact with life,
That strove to break my pact with love and death.
Nor shall I blame him ever with my breath,
And thus with blame set self with self at strife.
Enough, that he is wed, and I am not his wife.

LXXV

"There is an island off the Breton shore,
Small, and as simple as the lowly folk
From whose rude roofs up-curls the turf-fed smoke.
Sometimes the waves against it rage and roar,
Sometimes they kiss its feet, and woo it, and adore.

LXXVI

" Upon it is a little church-like shed,
Girt with a cluster of green nameless graves,
Green, but withal as billowy as the waves,
Yet just as motionless as those whose bed
Lies deep within, secure from trouble overhead.

LXXVII

" But one grave is there, shaped and smoothed with
care,
That bears a name, engraven deep and plain,
On a small granite slab without a stain ;
A name—no more—if fanciful, yet fair,
That looks up to the stars, and claimeth kindred there.

LXXVIII

" And in it do I often creep, and lie
Warm by my blossom that is cold within,
And faded ere it sorrow knew or sin.
Six summers did it gladden earth and sky
With carol and with song,—a bird, a butterfly.

LXXIX

" Then ceased both song and flight their brief sweet
span,
And all my prayers, and tears, and kisses, then,
Could coax it not to kiss me back again,
Nor call life's hues to temples white and wan :
And from that hour it was Love's Widowhood began.

LXXX

" For while it frolicked in and out the door,
Or nestled in my lap, outworn with play,
I somehow felt He was not far away,
But might at any moment come once more,
And love and all things be as they had been before.

LXXXI

" Fondling its curls, I used to close mine eyes,
And dimly fancy I was fondling his ;
And when its little lips my lips did kiss,
My heart would swell, and then subside, with sighs,
And soul and senses float on murmured lullabies.

LXXXII

" But when its fairy form no more was blown
Along the wind, nor gleamed athwart the grass,
Nor longer in its little crib, alas !
Glowed like a moist musk-rosebud newly blown,
Then knew I, night and day would find me still alone.

LXXXIII

" There was a gentle venerable priest,
Who had loved it with a yearning ofttimes shown
By those that have no kindred of their own ;
A love that is by sense of want increased,
And felt the most by hearts that taste of it the least.

LXXXIV

"And piously he wept, and soothed my hand,
And oft besought, and aided, me to pray.
But since his sole joy now was ta'en away,
Shortly he followed it to death's dim land,
And he too sleeps in peace beside the Breton strand.

LXXXV

"None then were left who loved my blossom save
Two snowy-wimpled nuns, that, tender-eyed,
Smiled while it lived and sorrowed when it died.
But they were bidden elsewhere, and one lone grave
My sole companion now, with wailings of the wave.

LXXXVI

"Then with tears bitter as the salt sea-brine,
And which, like sea-mist, blotted out my gaze,
I came back to these quiet woodland ways,
Where, in my youth, I dreamed my dream divine,
And which must still remain for ever his and mine."

LXXXVII

She ceased : and I could hear a chestnut fall
From branch to branch, then drop upon the ground,
And in the slowly purpling air the sound
Of the first rooks returning to the Hall
From seaward marshy lands, and answering call with call.

LXXXVIII

Thuswise we listened; neither having speech
To mate the silence. But she knew my heart
Was nearer to her now, not more apart,
Since that sad story of the Breton beach,
And yearned still more toward hers, which still it could
  not reach.

LXXXIX

When next I thither bent my steps, I found
A something, heretofore I had not seen,
Almost akin to sunshine in her mien;
A cheerful gravity that hovered round
The face of things, and drank content from sight and
  sound.

XC

"Welcome!" she said, "and welcome more to-day
Than ever yet, though welcome always here.
For we must do the service of the Year,
That kind taskmaster whom we both obey,
And whom we serve for love, whom others serve for pay.

XCI

"His need is very pressing, for behold!
The ruddy apples bend the branches down,
Like children tugging at their mother's gown.
There are all colours, russet, red, and gold,
Pippins of every sort, and codlins manifold.

XCII

"On their sweet pulp the thievish jackdaws browse,
And leave the half-pecked fruit upon the ground,
To nibble at the others plump and sound.
The wasps fall drowsy-drunk from off the boughs,
Or zigzag to their nests, to sleep off their carouse.

XCIII

"Look! I have donned my apron with the hem
Of primrose tint to please your April taste,
And primrose-purfled basket. Now, make haste,
And let us to the orchard,—branch and stem
Will soon be thick with thieves,—and be before with
    them.

XCIV

"Bring you the ladder from the lodge; the crates
Are ranged already round the oldest trees.
Shall we not be as busy as the bees,
And gather yet more honey? Harvest waits,
And we, since hired, must stand not idle at the gates."

XCV

Thereon I did her errand, and we went
With faces eager as our feet, to where
The juicy apples flavoured all the air;
And, on a trunk the ladder having leant,
I swarmed into the boughs, contenting and content.

XCVI

And all the afternoon there did I pluck
The ripe and rounded fruit, and when mayhap
I found one lustrous fair, into her lap
I flung it down, exclaiming, " Bite and suck
Its sweetness with your own, and leave me half for luck."

XCVII

And so she did, not making kind unkind,
Or natural strange, by being grossly coy.
In all my life I never had such joy.
Like water wimpled by a sunlit wind,
I plain could see her face smile-dimpled by her mind.

XCVIII

Nor till the crimson-flushing sky o'erhead
Seemed to have caught the colour of the fruit
That lay in circles round each gnarlëd root,
Stayed we our task ; and then we turned our tread
Back to the porch, since there her homeward fancy led.

XCIX

She passed within, but I remained without ;
And slowly felt, as there I sat apart,
The pain that sometimes comes about the heart
When we have been too happy, and the doubt
If joy like that can last puts timid hope to rout.

C

Shortly I heard her voice, " Are you there ?" she said,
And came and sat beside me.   From her face,
As from the sky the sunset light, all trace
Of late reflected happiness had fled,
And with a muffled voice she murmured, " He is dead."

CI

A letter lay upon her lap, but I
Looked not at it, nor her, but fixed my gaze,
As hers I knew was fixed, on far-off days,
When she was in her girlhood ; and the sky
Darkened, and one bright star beheld us from on high.

CII

I took her hand : she took it not away :
And in the twilight, which, when day is done,
Can make the past and present feel like one,
I found a free unfaltering voice to say
All that had filled my heart, full many an autumn day,

CIII

" He is not dead ; he lives ; he never died,
And never did desert you.   For you clung
Fast to his image, listened for his tongue,
Never a moment drifted from his side,
But shrined him in your heart, haloed and glorified.

CIV

" Thus he you loved was loyal, trustful, true,
As man tenacious, tender as a maid,
And of no fate save infamy afraid.
Nay, he was leal and loving even as you,
And what in you were base, that baseness could not do.

CV

" Loving him, yet you thought of him as one
Who still would love you though you loved him not,
And would remember even if you forgot ;
To be your shadow, needed not the sun,
But straight would hold his course, though hope of
  bourne was none.

CVI

" And such a one there is who loves you now,
And who will always love you, come what may.
Was it not therefore he you loved alway ?
No new love this, only an ancient vow,
Mellowed to fruit which then was blossom on the bough.

CVII

" Sweet, dear ! is youth, and sweet the days that bring
The wildwood's smile and cuckoo's wandering voice,
And all that bids us revel and rejoice.
But Autumn fosters, 'neath its folded wing,
A deeper love and joy than glimmer round the Spring."

CVIII

The silence moved not.   In the dewy air
The twilight deepened, and the stars came down,
And clustered round and round us like a crown.
I knew not if they circled here or there,
For Earth and Heaven were one, revolving everywhere.

CIX

I could not tell the sweetness from the smart,
Nor if the warm mist on my cheek were tears
From her loved lids or dewdrops from the Spheres.
There was no space for thought of things apart,
As her surrendered heart lay havened on my heart.

CX

And never again did gloom or cloud appear
While Autumn lingered in that happy land,
Where we still wandered, but now hand in hand;
Watching the woodmen in the copses clear
Broad rings of space and close the cycle of the year.

CXI

But long before the ringing of the axe
Was hushed by silences of silvery frost,
The threshold of the village church we crossed,
And stood, with downcast eyes and bending backs,
Before a scroll that bore the twin words, *Lux et Pax.*

CXII

And children's hands had tenderly arrayed
Harvest Thanksgiving, that auspicious morn,
Round rail, and arch, and column; blades of corn,
Garlands of rustic fruit, with leaves decayed,
And here and there a flower found in some sheltered
    glade.

CXIII

And children's voices shepherded the rite
That sanctified love's birth, and children strewed
Sweet-smelling herbs, thyme, box, and southernwood,
Under our feet, to augur us delight;
And children's eyes they were that watched us fade from
    sight.

CXIV

And we are going to the Breton shore,
Together by a little grave to weep,
And place fresh flowers around an angel's sleep.
For I am living in her life before,
And She, she lives in mine, both now and evermore.

CXV

So I who oft have carolled of the Spring,
Now chant of Autumn and the fruitful days;
Of windless dawns enveiled in dewy haze,
Of cloistered evenings when no loud birds sing,
But Love in silence broods, with fondly-folded wing.

Printed by R. & R. CLARK, *Edinburgh*

MESSRS. MACMILLAN AND CO.'S PUBLICATIONS.

Now Publishing in Monthly Volumes.
Crown 8vo, Cloth, 5s. each.

A COLLECTED EDITION

OF

THE POETICAL WORKS OF
MR. ALFRED AUSTIN

Vol. I. THE TOWER OF BABEL: A CELESTIAL
LOVE STORY.

Vol. II. SAVONAROLA: A TRAGEDY.

Vol. III. PRINCE LUCIFER.

Vol. IV. THE HUMAN TRAGEDY.

Vol. V. NARRATIVE POEMS

Vol. VI. LYRICAL POEMS.

MACMILLAN AND CO., LONDON.

www.ingramcontent.com/pod-product-compliance
Lightning Source LLC
Chambersburg PA
CBHW030553040726
47497CB00008B/2697